FORBIDDEN

Love in London, Book 1

LAUREN SMITH

Lauren Smith (signature)

Lauren
SMITH
TIMELESS ROMANCE

Copyright © 2016 by Lauren Smith

This book was Previously Published in 2016 by Hachette Book Group USA and is now republished by Lauren Smith Books in 2018

Cover design by Cover Couture

Stock Photography: Depositphotos/Yurkaimmortal

Shutterstock/Olavs

ISBN: 978-1-947206-64-9 (ebook)

ISBN: 978-1-947206-45-8 (Trade paperback)

OTHER TITLES BY LAUREN
SMITH

To the little pub just outside of Magdalene College, where the spark of so many stories was ignited.

ACKNOWLEDGMENTS

I'd like to thank Claire for being my "go-to" gal for all things English. You're a wonderful friend for putting up with my silly e-mails about how modern Brits would do or say things. For Amanda, Chrissy, Jeanne, Angela, Amy, and Liz, beta readers and good friends who always help me make my stories sparkle and shine.

I

"**T**onight is the start of my grand adventure. And since it's my birthday, you guys are welcome to join in the fun." Kat Roberts grinned as she spread out the folded piece of paper on the table so her friends Lacy and Mark could see.

They were nestled in the corner of the Pickerel Inn just outside Magdalene College in Cambridge, catching a brief break from studying for exams. The pub was full of other students, all enjoying the relaxed atmosphere and the fish and chips the pub served late into the night.

"What on earth is that?" Lacy asked as she brushed her hair back from her face and peered at the list.

Kat tapped the paper. "A list of ten things every undergraduate should do while studying and living in Cambridge. Number one? Drink a glass of Nelson's Revenge at the Pickerel Inn pub on Magdalene Street."

Mark, Lacy's boyfriend, chuckled. "Have too many Nelsons and he'll definitely get his revenge. You Americans aren't used to our stout ales."

Kat was only half-listening as she studied the list, contemplating the other suggestions it gave. She'd moved to England in August to start college while her dad worked in London, and now more than ever she wanted to do something wild, something fun and crazy. Her parents had divorced when she was a kid, and she'd been living with her father, whose job entailed frequent corporate moves. She'd been too afraid to get close to people and break out of her shell. She didn't want to make connections with people only to have to leave and never see them again. It reminded her too much of when her mother had left.

But that's all changed. I'm finally living in one place for three years. I'm making friends here. Roots. For the first time I can really live.

Now she yearned for an adventure. She wasn't used to being wild and crazy or doing things out of her comfort zone, but she wanted to be that way.

Baby steps, she had to remind herself. That's why she'd picked this list from an online article about attending school in Cambridge. It had fun things for her to do. Things she might not have otherwise tried. Now that she'd settled into her classes and schoolwork, she could focus on enjoying the whole college experience. She'd picked an easy item from the list first—drinking a pint here at the Pickerel—but she'd work her way up to the bigger items soon.

Mark leaned forward, his elbows propped on the old wooden table. "Is this really all we get to do to help you celebrate your nineteenth birthday?"

"He's right, Kat. We should be doing something really fun tonight. Like going clubbing!" Lacy curved her lips in a charming but teasing smile that under other circumstances would've made Kat laugh.

"Clubbing? Lacy, you know I can't dance. I'd fall flat on my face. Maybe if I drink enough you can talk me into it." Kat winked at her friend and gulped down more of the cider and beer blend she had ordered. It wasn't strong, but she wanted to get warmed up before going for the Nelson's Revenge.

Lacy grinned. "You're officially nineteen, and as this is your first semester at college, we need to make something amazing happen. Leave high school behind. This is your chance. Let's go dancing, meet some hot guys." She jerked her head suggestively toward a nearby table where a group of decent-looking men were watching them, pints in hand and friendly smiles on their faces. She nudged Mark in the ribs. "Right?" She winked.

Mark put an arm around Lacy's shoulders and shook his head, silently laughing. "You have a hot guy right here for you, no need to find a new one," he teased.

Lacy rolled her eyes. "You know what I mean, *for Kat*. She needs some action."

Kat couldn't disagree. She'd never really dated in high school since she and her dad had moved every couple of years. Maybe Lacy was right. Now was the time to give it a try.

"First I'll drink my pint, then I'll work my way up to meeting hot guys. How's that?"

Mark shook his head. "I think you're underestimating your appeal. British blokes like me would love to date an American. You'll have no trouble getting a guy." He nodded at the same group of men his girlfriend had pointed out. "Start with them. They look nice enough, and if they aren't, I'll beat them up for you." Mark put up his fists with a silly, goonish expression that made Kat and Lacy giggle.

Kat adored her new friends. She'd only known them since August, but something about them, their natural warmth, the way they opened up to her, made her feel like she'd known them for years.

Maybe it was the magic of the city, too. Ever since she'd come here for university, this little Elizabethan-era town had captivated her. Between the shops tucked in crooked, wandering alleys and the tolling bells of the various colleges throughout the day, Kat had been bewitched by this tiny part of the world. It was more of a home for her than any other place she'd ever lived.

"Well, don't tell me you're afraid to give it a go?" Mark laughed.

His brown eyes were dark and full of brotherly mischief, offering a friendship Kat hadn't thought she'd find again since she'd left her last high school boyfriend behind. She and Ben had been good friends, more than she'd ever thought possible with a guy. Like him, Mark was easygoing, with a ready smile and a playful attitude that put her at ease.

She and Ben hadn't been serious, and calling him a boyfriend was really more of a stretch. They'd hung out but never even kissed. When she'd confessed this to Lacy, her friend had gasped and immediately informed her that what she and Ben hadn't been a "real" relationship.

Kat jerked herself out of the spiral her thoughts had taken and focused on her friends. She tipped back her drink and finished it. She couldn't believe it was close to the end of November, and the term was winding down. As much as she'd enjoyed her classes, she was glad for the upcoming winter break. What better way to start the holidays than getting a jump-start on her "Operation Adventure."

When the front door of the pub suddenly opened, an icy wind cut through the cozy atmosphere of the building. Despite the dim gold light cast by the fixtures in the pub, Kat could see more than one person at the surrounding tables muttering, clutching at their coats and glancing toward the front door.

"Oh my," Lacy murmured, her brown eyes all soft and dreamy as she stared at something behind Kat.

Mark coughed, catching Lacy's attention, but Kat was already turning around in her seat. For some reason all of the breath left her body and she blinked, completely spellbound.

There, framed in the doorway, was a living, breathing god. When he closed the door behind him, snowflakes swirled and eddied around him, clinging to his dark hair and his black knee-length pea coat. He made her think of Hades, the dark god of the Netherworld, in search of his sweet, innocent lover Persephone.

Kat would never have thought she'd describe a man in such terms, but this man...oh yes, the description was perfect. So perfect it almost hurt to look at him. The kind of gorgeous that made a woman's body respond instantly. A slow wave of heat overtook Kat as she stared at him, and she clamped her thighs together when a slow throb began to build in her lower abdomen.

Now that's the sort of man I want to get involved with. One who would sweep me away, make me forget who I used to be, and show me who I might become. A woman who lives life on the edge, who explores dark passions and truly experiences life. The thought of being with a man like him... it felt right to want him.

The decent-looking guys a few tables away had nothing on this man. And that was just it: He was a man. Nothing about him screamed "college student." The way he walked, in an almost predatory, graceful movement, sucked her in, and she couldn't look away. He was the sort of man who would stop every woman in her tracks as he strode past, demanding their attention, *their desire*...

His eyes swept over the room, not even noticing her.

No surprise. She was just another undergraduate

student bundled up in jeans, a thick sweater, and boots.

Not like him.

A pinch of pain in her chest made her set her cider down and blink rapidly. She'd never minded being invisible before, but looking at this sexy god of a man...she wanted to get his attention. It was a stupid, girlish feeling, but she wanted him to look her way, see her. The pull he had on her was strange, magnetic, like nothing she'd ever felt before. It was as though something inside her was pulling her toward him, erasing everything else around him.

Look my way, she silently begged.

But he didn't. A knot of disappointment tightened in her chest. There was no way he'd ever notice her.

He's way out of my league. We're in different galaxies.

Even knowing this, she couldn't stop looking at him. This man looked expensive, from his shiny, black boots to the sleek look of his trousers and coat. When her gaze locked on his face, she was lost in a study of him. His aristocratic features were stunning. The man had a jawline that looked like it had been cut from marble, and a straight patrician nose that created an aura of entitled ease. He knew he was attractive and exactly how his mere presence could affect a room.

The hint of an arrogant smile played upon his full, sensual lips, so faint that she wondered if she was imagining it. And there was something about how he surveyed the room, like a ruler among his subjects. It wasn't surprising. Like King Arthur, but with dark, chocolate hair rather than fair. He was tall and lean with wide shoulders, and she could tell there were muscles beneath those fine clothes by the way the fabric clung to him. As he strode over to the bar and leaned against it to order a drink, the focus of the room went with him.

A stir of whispers started up a table behind Kat, Lacy, and Mark. A group of college students, three girls, were watching the new stranger, too. Their heads were bent together, and their hushed voices carried just enough that Kat caught snippets of their conversation.

"I think that's....yes, I'm sure it's him. You go, Talia, ask him..." one girl suggested.

"No way, if that's who he is...He'd never...Too hot though right? I'd let him do anything to me..." More giggles. "Can you imagine having sex with him? I heard he's a god in bed. I'd like Mr. Sexy to take me home."

The third girl fanned herself. "He's got a bad reputation, though...total heartbreaker. Never dates, only fucks them, you know...but I'll be damned if I don't want to..."

The conversation was muffled when a waiter delivered the girls more beers, and Kat couldn't hear anything else. So whoever Mr. Sexy was...these girls knew him or knew *of him*. And he had a bad reputation? What kind of bad reputation?

Kat turned her focus back to him, gazing longingly, watching him slide his black leather gloves off to reveal long fingers and elegant but masculine hands. A gold signet ring gleamed on the little finger of his left hand. She swallowed hard as a wave of heat rippled through her so fast beads of sweat gathered at her temples. She reached for her empty glass of cider again, never taking her eyes off the gorgeous man.

"You should probably go get your pint of Nelson's Revenge," Lacy said. "I really want to go clubbing, so get that drink, check it off your list, and let's go!"

Her friend's voice seemed to break through the odd sort of fog in her head. She didn't want to leave this little pub and go dancing, not when a man like *him* was here. She could have watched him all night.

Clubbing was definitely not on the list of things she'd like to do, but it would get her out of her shell. Of course, it would really help if she had that drink. And getting that drink meant a chance to get close to the beautiful stranger.

"Okay, be back in a second." She pushed her chair and headed toward the bar. The crowd was thick around the bartender, and Kat could barely see him over the heads of the students laughing and talking as they leaned against the antique wood bar. The only empty spot against the counter was next to Mr. Sexy...

Raising her chin, she started to walk in his direction, attempting to play it cool, like she wasn't going to get turned on just by standing so close to this god of a man.

He probably won't even look at me...but what if he does? Gotta be cool....I can handle this, right?

A second before she reached him, her right foot slipped in a spot of melted snow.

"Ahh!" Kat gasped as she tried to catch herself, but she careened straight into the beautiful stranger. Normally she wouldn't have been so clumsy, but she'd been too focused on him and hadn't been watching the floor. Plenty of people had been slipping all night.

"Oomph," he grunted and threw his arms out, pulling her to his chest.

Kat's head fell back as she clung to his shoulders. He was tall, deliciously so, and her head only just reached the bottom of his chin. His hair was swept back from his face, but it fell across his eyes as he stared down at her, and the light kissed the dark brown strands with a faint hint of gold. The color of his eyes was...stunning and made her almost dizzy when she stared. Like losing herself in a kaleidoscope of blue and green in endless splintering shafts.

Her knees wobbled, and she dug her hands harder into his shoulders, trying to stay on her feet.

What is wrong with me?

"Hello, darling, are you all right? Bit of a slick spot, eh?"

That rich voice, such decadent, sinful syllables uttered in that oh-so-perfect English accent, made Kat quiver inside. What was it about accents? They made a girl think strange, silly things, like asking him to talk dirty to her. Oh, the things he could say that would melt her into a puddle just like the snow at his feet. It might kill her with pleasure. The thought was so unlike her that she blinked. There was something about this man that made her want things she'd been hesitant to want before now. Like hot, sweaty sex. She was still a virgin, and yet this man was making her want to strip down naked and jump into the nearest bed with him.

"I..."

His hands were still holding her waist, his body pressed against hers. She couldn't think; her brain short-circuited. His hands on her, so hot to the touch...They were standing so close, faces mere inches apart, and the world around her seemed to burn with a heat along her skin. Her breath quickened.

Kat struggled to think logically, but all she could think about was how much she wanted to kiss him.

"Are you able to stand on your own?" He smiled, the single flirty twist of his lips making her knees buckle again.

What the heck? She'd never had a problem with her legs working before.

"Er...yes," she finally managed to say.

"Good." His hands dropped, but the movement

felt reluctant. He trailed his hands down her body, the light but suggestive skimming of his palms over her waist, then her hips, sent little throbbing pulses throughout her entire body. He didn't step away, either, but kept close to her, his eyes still fixed on her face. "I'm glad to have prevented a nasty fall."

Before she could reply, the bartender leaned over the counter and spoke. "What can I get you?"

Mr. Tall and Sexy shifted slightly, allowing Kat to slip into the space next to him, their shoulders and arms touching as she answered.

"I'll have a pint of Nelson's Revenge, please."

The stranger next to her chuckled. "Are you sure about that?" he asked. "That's a stiff drink and likely to bring tears to your eyes." There was a hint of teasing in his tone, and Kat couldn't resist responding.

"I'm sure. Besides, I'm more likely to start crying at the sight of a butterfly than a stout ale." She laughed, then realized what'd she said and blushed.

The man angled his body toward her, propping one arm on the counter as he stared down at her.

"Butterflies make you cry? What on earth for? Don't tell me you're afraid of them." Humor heated those blue-green eyes of his, and she felt an answering heat sweep through her body.

"I...well, it's silly really..." She hedged. She didn't normally open up to people, let alone strange, beautiful men in pubs. But there was something about the way he was watching her, his intense focus on her and his interest in what she was saying, that gave her courage to continue.

"I used to live in Texas with my dad, and we saw monarch butterflies when they migrated. But now with their habitats dying out, I rarely see them. When I do get lucky and one flies past me, it's beautiful...and sad." She shrugged her shoulders, glancing away. "I know that sounds silly."

"Not at all," he murmured softly. "No sillier than how I feel when I look at stained glass windows. It's the same for me, that mixture of melancholy and beauty. It's not often I meet someone else who thinks about things like that." His intense scrutiny tore her in two directions, between the need to squirm and to go very still.

The man possessed an overpowering, seductive and masculine presence. She caught the scent of pine and something clean and crisp that sparked her other senses to life. It encompassed her like some dark spell, leaving her with a desperate need to stay close to him. The things those girls had whispered about him came rushing back..."*bad reputation*"..."*god in bed*"...Whoever he was didn't matter, she just *wanted* him. Wanted to curl her arms around his neck and get as close to him as possible.

"I think about that stuff all the time," she said, unable to tear her gaze away from his.

He lifted his glass to his lips and sipped. It wasn't ale he was drinking but something else, a dark, warm gold color, probably Scotch. She realized she must have been staring at his mouth when he licked his lips and spoke again.

"Keep staring at me like that and I'm liable to kiss you."

Desire and hunger lit up his eyes, heating the strange mixture of blue and green. It almost made her forget that she was talking to a stranger. It *really* was possible to lose yourself in someone's eyes. Maybe the poets weren't wrong about love at first sight. She didn't love this man, but she was...captivated by him, which felt like love, in a strange sort of way. The lightness of her head, the wobbly knees, the fascination with him.

"There's nothing stopping you from kissing me," she breathed. Her heart was pounding against her ribs as excitement skittered through her. Would he accept the challenge and kiss her?

His eyes softened, but there was a dangerous glint to his expression, one that warned her that if he kissed her...it wouldn't be chaste, wouldn't be sweet. It would be the sort of kiss that made a girl forget where she was and moan helplessly for more.

They were mere inches apart now...When had she leaned into him? Somehow she had shifted closer, fixated on his mouth, the full sensual lips. The bit of the cider ale she'd been drinking earlier made her thoughts a bit muddy. Well, all but one thought.

I want him to kiss me. If he won't, I'll kiss him first.

Before she let herself think better of it, she seized the chance to be reckless and rocked up on her tip-toes, curling her fingers into the lapels of his coat as she kissed him. *Hard*. It was wild, the way she let go and just gave herself into kissing him. Her own sexy stranger...

His hands gripped her waist, fingers digging in slightly, making tingles of excitement shoot down her spine, clear to her toes. His lips were soft and warm, moving against hers hungrily. When he angled his face, he caressed her lips with his tongue. The star-tling, erotic feel of it had her mouth parting, and he thrust inside. The little teasing strokes of his tongue against hers created shivers deep in her belly. He overwhelmed all of her senses, and Kat couldn't catch her breath. There was no escaping his strong hold, and she didn't want to. His lips were a drug, and she couldn't get enough.

Every cell in her body pulsed and hummed to life when the kiss turned slightly rough, as he nipped her bottom lip. She rocked her body into his, desperate to get closer, to feel him completely surrounding her.

All mine. She smiled against his lips just as their bodies separated a few inches and she gasped for a breath. Blood pounded against her temples, and she panted and glanced up at him. Stark, raw lust burned like coals behind his eyes as he stared down at her, an almost animal ferocity in his expression.

"That was—"

Before she could finish, he curled an arm around her waist and pulled her flush against him for another kiss. The touch of his lips this time was feather light...as though he were savoring her. A simple, al-most innocent brush of mouths, before she shivered, and a little moan of longing escaped. Suddenly he ro-tated her, pinning her against the bar, his mouth taking her hungrily, seeking entrance to hers. She parted her lips, more from surprise than anything else. When his tongue slid in and teased hers, she whimpered. The bare hint of stubble rasped against her skin as he kissed her, making her sensitive to every sensation.

More, I need more of this...

No one she'd dated in high school had kissed like this, as though he had all night to taste her, explore her, excite her. Nothing else mattered, nothing but this man and his life-altering, seductive lips.

When his mouth parted from hers, she blinked and stared up at him, wondrously dazed.

"You were too tempting to resist. Makes a man hungry for more when a woman looks at him like that." He brushed the pad of his thumb over her swollen lips, his eyes tracing the shape, along with his finger.

"Like what?" she asked, fascinated by his words just as much as his hands and the way they touched her.

His laugh was dark and rich like a pint of Guinness. "Like she needs to be kissed, to be *taken* by a man who knows just what to do to make her moan with pleasure."

Taken...the word was heavy, dark, forbidding and yet it filled her with a secret thrill. She could picture this man taking her, doing a thousand erotic things that would blow her mind and her body apart.

She struggled to respond, but what could she say to the man who'd just changed her life with one mind-blowing kiss and talked to her about how he could make a woman moan with pleasure? Had she really just made out with a complete and total stranger? She needed to do something, *anything*, to lessen the suddenly awkward moment.

She thrust out her hand and said, "I'm Katherine Roberts, but everyone calls me Kat." It felt silly to introduce herself after the kiss they'd shared, but she did it anyway.

The man stared at her hand and then took it, raising it to his lips rather than shaking it. He brushed his mouth over the backs of her knuckles in a caress, like an old world prince greeting a lady. Her heart fluttered inside her chest at the little romantic act. She'd never met a man who'd done that before, and it made her imagine what it might feel like to have his lips on other parts of her body.

"Tristan Kingsley. It's been quite the pleasure meeting you." The blue-green of his eyes rippled with glints of light like a summer lake at noon. "I'd like to kiss you again—"

"Tristan! There you are!" A light, feminine voice shook Kat out of her hazy daydreams of being wrapped in his arms again.

A tall blonde with stunning, classical features and a killer sense of style stood in the pub's doorway, watching Tristan and Kat. Her pink lips were curved up in an excited smile, and her blue eyes were bright and merry.

"So sorry I'm late. The snow is quite wretched on the roads," she said as she strode over in her too per-fect high-heeled boots and skinny jeans.

Kat wanted to melt into the floor but shuffled her own scuffed boots instead. Her face heated when Tristan released her hand and glanced at the blonde woman. Just like that, Kat was forgotten as he stepped around her. So much for her dreams of a man like that paying attention to her. She was just another passing fancy while he waited for his girlfriend to show up. A wave of nausea mixed with anxiety rolled through her stomach. This was why she was afraid to take risks. Because rejection hurt like hell.

"Celia!" Tristan grinned, as he opened his arms to embrace the beautiful woman.

Oh, God. She really is his girlfriend. Of course she is. Tristan looked perfect with Celia. It was obvious they were a couple. A couple of beautiful, sophisticated people. Like a pair of models from a Burberry ad. She'd never had a snowball's chance in hell with a guy like him.

Kat slipped away, her pint of Nelson's Revenge in her hands as she left Tristan and headed back to her friends. Mark and Lacy were watching her when she dropped down into her seat and covered her face with her hand.

"Wow, Kat, that was..." Lacy reached out and gave Kat's shoulder a pat.

"Mortifying? Pathetic?" Kat supplied, as she finally dropped her hand from her face and set her glass down next to Mark, nudging it in his direction. Drinking the pint seemed to pale in comparison to the adventure of being kissed by Tristan Kingsley.

"Well, the kiss was kind of hot...until that other girl showed up," Mark observed with a smirk, but he had a point.

She'd been totally on fire and hadn't wanted to stop kissing Tristan. It was as though her life had depended on touching him, on feeling his muscles move beneath her hands, and his mouth exploring hers. There had been nothing else in the world she'd wanted more than him in that moment. She'd *never* felt like that before about anyone or anything.

"I know, right? What kind of guy kisses someone like that when he has a girlfriend?" Lacy said, crossing her arms over her chest.

Mark laughed. "Obviously that guy."

Kat winced. "Do you mind if I just go back to the dorm? I think I've had enough of this place tonight."

"But it's your birthday." Lacy pouted.

Kat shrugged. This was the first time she wasn't celebrating with her father. They'd moved from

Chicago to London in August and neither of them had thought about what it would mean when she was two hours away at Cambridge for her birthday. Somehow celebrating without him didn't feel right.

"What about cake?" Mark asked before drinking some of his pint.

"No, thanks." Kat shook her head and brushed some dust off the table, avoiding looking in Tristan's direction.

How was it possible to still feel his lips on hers when he was a dozen feet away?

"Are you sure?" Lacy asked, her brows knit together in concern.

"Yeah, I'm sure. I'd rather just go back to the dorms. I have a lot of studying ahead of me in the next couple of weeks before final exams."

"Well, drat," Lacy said. "All right, you go home, then." She nudged Mark. "Go pay for the drinks. It's on us tonight, Kat."

"Thanks, guys." Kat stood and tucked her chair under the wooden table. "See you both tomorrow?"

"Bright and early," Lacy laughed. "Did I ever say how much I hate 8:30 a.m. classes?"

Mark leaned over and kissed Lacy's cheek. "That's why I'm the smart one. My first class is never before 11 a.m."

"That's right, rub it in," Lacy grumbled, but she was smiling at him.

"Bye, guys." Kat was still laughing as she exited the pub. She didn't want to think about the mysterious Tristan Kingsley or how he kissed. Better to just forget it and move on. It had been a fun adventure, even if a short one.

The snow blew in thick currents around her, and the dim streetlights looked like glowing golden orbs in the darkness. It was a bewitching sight.

Most of the small shops around the pub were

closed, but one was still open. Its merry lights called to her as she approached. A bakery. Cakes, breads, and other sweets filled the windows. Behind the glass counter, a plump woman was checking a tray of cookies, the front of her blue apron dusted with small white splotches of flour.

"Maybe just one," Kat murmured, entranced by the sight of the small chocolate cupcakes with elaborate swirls of icing. It was her birthday, after all. Kat entered the shop and the brass bell above her head tinkled.

"Hello, dearie," the woman said and wiped flour-covered hands on her apron. "Come to get a late-night snack? You're just in time, I was ready to close up early due to the weather."

Kat peered through the glass cases, trying to decide which one of the little cakes would taste as good as the man she'd kissed only minutes ago. She doubted anything could come close.

Tristan. Tristan who had a girlfriend. Kat mentally kicked herself. She'd pretty much thrown herself at him and begged to be kissed. Maybe he didn't normally go around slipping his tongue between a girl's lips and setting her on fire inside. Then again...if he'd been a good guy, he wouldn't have done more than a chaste peck on the cheek.

Focus on chocolate, not hot Brit you'll never see again. She went back to studying the contents of the case. When the entry bell clinked again, she didn't turn around.

"Have a need for something sweet?" A rich, decadent voice, smooth as chocolate, filled her ears.

She spun to find Tristan standing there, snow dancing about him as he let the door close behind him. He walked toward her with lithe, graceful steps. Her body trembled with a little wave of excitement at the mere sight of him. *I shouldn't be happy to see him, he* *has a girlfriend...*But that didn't change the rapid beat of her heart.

"Evening," the baker said merrily.

"What are you doing here?" Kat sputtered. The moment the words were out, she slapped a hand over her mouth.

His chuckle made a warm flush creep down her cheeks. "I saw you left the pub and..." He paused, his brows drawing together. "Well, I didn't want you to go off on your own. I saw that your friends remained behind." It was a lame excuse, and they both knew it. For some reason that made her want to smile.

"So you're protecting me from snowflakes?" She couldn't help the partly amused and partly sarcastic tone of her voice.

Tristan shrugged and joined her at the counter, peering at the desserts. "Snowflakes can be treacherous buggers."

This time she couldn't stop her laugh. "I'll bet. Death by ice fractals sounds horrifying."

He quirked a brow. "Ice fractals?"

God, I'm an idiot. Sure, Kat, show him what a nerd you are. "They're the mathematical phenomena of a repeating pattern that displays on every scale. Snowflakes are one of nature's fractals." She wasn't a science wiz, but learning was something she enjoyed, no matter what subject. Ben had always teased her about it. Not that she'd minded being called a nerd. There were worse things than being addicted to learning.

Tristan glanced over his shoulder at the dancing snow, then turned back to her. "I'm surprised you know what fractals are. Most people don't." He leaned forward then and caught a lock of her hair, playing with the strands. Kat held her breath as every nerve in her tingled to life. He was touching her again, and she could feel every cell of her body humming with excitement.

Please kiss me again.

When he didn't, her mind attempted to return to reality, and she remembered Celia.

"What about your girlfriend?" she blurted out.

"Girlfriend?" He let her hair drop from his fingers and met her gaze.

"That woman in the pub..." *The one he looked so perfect standing next to.*

"Celia?" The responding smile that lit his face filled her with envy. Would a man ever smile like that when he thought about her? Something about Tristan and the way he smiled, she couldn't help but wish one smile was for her.

"Right, Celia," she echoed. Her heart twinged a little at the mention of the other woman.

"She's my cousin, not my girlfriend."

Kat stared. This total stranger had abandoned his cousin to chase after her? Tiny flutters of excitement stirred in her stomach.

"You seem surprised." His sensual lips—lips she couldn't get out of her mind—twitched, as though he was fighting off a smile.

"Why ditch your cousin when you don't even know me?" This entire evening was surreal. God-like men coming in from snowstorms to kiss her senseless...What next? Winning the lottery and moving to the Bahamas?

Tristan's gaze dropped to her mouth.

"When a lovely woman kisses me and runs off into the snowy night...well, the temptation to go after her is irresistible. I don't let lovely women escape, not until I've tasted them properly." He licked his lips and everything south of her waist throbbed to life.

What? Was he kidding?

"So here I am, in a bakery with you. Is there a

reason we're staring at cakes?" He moved a step closer, even though he was facing the desserts again.

His arm brushed her right shoulder. The man was tall, but not too tall. Just enough to make a girl feel small, in a good way, like he could protect her if she needed it. A masculine scent, warm and clean, filled her nose. *His* scent. It was an enticing one she could've inhaled forever.

Focus, Kat. Try to be normal and have a normal conversation. Do not keep starting at Mr. Sexy.

"It's my birthday today. I'm nineteen."

At her reply, he looked at her again.

"Well, we must get you a cake. Chocolate, I presume?" He leaned one elbow on the glass counter as he waited for her to answer.

She nodded mutely.

Tristan turned back to the woman behind the counter. "What's the best chocolate cake you have? The richest, most decadent one." His words were as decadent as his statement. She could practically feel the chocolate melting on her tongue.

"The Devil's Triple Layer Cake." The woman pulled out a small cake for two people. Raspberry sauce was drizzled over the top of the simple yet elegant icing design.

Tristan took out his wallet and slid a black credit card across the counter.

"We'll take it. And a small candle, if you have one."

"**B**ut—" Kat's protest died when the woman took the Devil's cake from the counter and started to box it up. She didn't like feeling indebted to him, and he'd already made her feel off balance with his kisses.

"Consider it a thank-you." He laughed.

"For what?" Her tone was a breathless as she watched his dark hair fall into his eyes. Her hands twitched to brush it back from his face, to touch him back the way he'd so boldly touched her earlier. Everything about this man drew her in—his face, his eyes, his rich voice speaking of kisses and passion.

"You surprised me tonight. It's been a long time since anyone has done that." He scrubbed a hand over his jaw, and she saw the hint of stubble there and remembered the way it had tickled her when she'd kissed him.

I surprised myself, kissing him like that.

"Allow me to escort you home. Is it a long walk?" Tristan asked Kat, when the woman had returned with the boxed cake.

"Only a block. I'm staying in a dorm at Magdalene. College." She shouldn't be telling him something like that. What if he got the wrong idea?

"A student at university? Excellent. So am I." He smiled. "I'm not an undergraduate, though. I'm earning a Master's degree in business." He thanked the baker and collected the box with the cake. "I'll walk you home." It was a statement this time, not a question, and she didn't want to argue with him, not when it meant spending more time in his presence. She'd just have to be sure he didn't think she'd...well, she'd worry about that when they got to her dorm.

"You're a student? How old are you?" Kat could've smacked herself for being so rude. "I'm sorry, I shouldn't have asked."

"I'm twenty-five." He held the door open with one hand, and she had to slide past him to exit the bakery. A gust carrying fresh snow hit her face, and she braced against the frigid air. Her first instinct was to turn around and bury herself against Tristan. He was so warm, she remembered from kissing him at the bar. The way his body had enveloped hers with heat, and the way his hands had gripped her hips.

"So what brings an American to Cambridge? Is this a semester of study abroad?" He walked alongside her as they went down the street, snow crunching beneath their feet. Kat stayed closer to Tristan than she would have normally, telling herself it was because she was afraid she'd slip on the ice. But the truth was that she wanted to be close to him, feel his warmth, smell that piney scent of his that made her senses come alive. She struggled to focus on their conversation, given how her thoughts kept drifting into dangerous territory.

"I'm a full-time student. My father travels for work, and he's living in London for the next couple of years."

Tristan made a little hum of interest. "And what does your father do?"

"He's an investment banker at Barclays. He's at

their London office, and I wanted to be close to him."
It was so easy to talk to Tristan. Maybe it was because
she knew she'd likely never see him again after
tonight. But it wasn't just that. Something about
talking to him just clicked.

It reminded her of a day when she'd been a young
girl, crawling through her parents' attic searching for
treasure maps and wardrobes that opened to snow-
swept worlds lit by solitary lampposts. She'd come
across a large, weather-beaten, locked trunk. After
hours of digging through boxes, she'd found an ornate
key in an antique lacquered jewelry box heavily covered with dust.

Eyeing the lock and the key, she'd given it a
chance. The satisfying click-click of the key in the
lock had made her heart pound and her hands
tremble as she'd opened the trunk. It had contained
old books, the very best kind, of course. But she'd
never forget the moment of fitting that key into
place, and the feeling of connectedness it had made.
Being near Tristan, talking to him, was like fitting
that key into the lock all over again, and she couldn't
fathom why that was, only that it was true. It scared
her a little, but she wasn't the kind of woman to turn
her back on something amazing just because it sent
her nerves skittering inside her.

"And your mother?" Tristan paused as they
reached the main door to her college grounds. The
massive, ten-foot-high door had a smaller door built
into its frame that everyone used to enter the
grounds. It was a bit like a scene from *Alice in Won-
derland*.

The smaller door to the college was unlocked, and
Kat entered, Tristan following behind her. A cheery
porter came out of his booth to greet them.

Tristan caught her arm, halting her in the middle
of the snowy courtyard so she had to face him. The

hold was firm, and the subtle sign of power rippling through that touch made her shiver. She remembered how he'd grabbed her in the pub, kissing her, forcing her to enjoy his kiss without escaping. It was madness to desire that, to let him take control and allow her the freedom to just...feel. But that was the thing about this man she couldn't get out of her head. If he could affect her in public, in a pub, what would it be like when they were completely alone?

"You didn't answer my question about your mother." There was a gentle reprimand in his voice. Their warm breaths billowed out in soft, white clouds in the Magdalene courtyard.

Those unique eyes of his held her spellbound. It was like watching the tide pulling out to sea and being sucked deeper into the water.

"I...my mother isn't part of my life, hasn't been for quite some time." For some reason, admitting that out loud stung. Thinking about the woman who'd abandoned her hurt, but saying it aloud made it too real, too painful. She and her father never talked about her mother and how empty her leaving had left Kat feeling. No one to talk to, bake with, laugh about boys with, see mushy romantic movies with...those were all the things mothers and daughters were supposed to do. *But not me.*

"I didn't mean to open old wounds, darling." Tristan's eyes softened, the colors changing yet again, and she was lost in their depths. The way he'd called her "*darling,*" that intimate word surrounded her heart with a cottony warmth. This beautiful stranger was offering her comfort, and she wanted it, wanted him. And that need scared her. She'd needed her mother, and her mother had left. The only person who hadn't let her down was her father. Kat couldn't let herself need Tristan, not when it might lead to more heartache.

He cupped her cheek, the gesture tender. How could he be such a contradiction? Bold and seductive, then tender and compassionate.

"They're divorced?" he asked. That focused intensity only seemed to deepen as the snowfall muffled the world around them. Like they were cocooned in the shelter of a snow globe holding only them and the falling white flakes.

She licked her lips. "Yes. For a long time now."

Tristan nodded. "My parents are divorced, as well. My father is an overbearing, pompous arse." He chuckled, but there was a bite to the sound that caught her attention.

"You don't like your father?" she asked.

The flash of cold in his eyes made her shiver more than the snow falling around them. He continued to stroke her cheek with one of his hands, which softened the hard look in his eyes.

"I don't like to talk about him." It was clear from the steel in his voice that she wouldn't get anything else from him about his father. But she wanted to know more about this mysterious, seductive stranger whose kisses burned straight through her. There were hidden depths to him, dark, deep, flowing underground rivers and she wanted to dive in and discover who he really was.

"What about your mother?"

The defensiveness evaporated as he grinned. "One of the best, as far as mothers go."

"That must be nice, to have a mother around, I mean." A part of her still felt like maybe *she* had been the cause of her parents' breakup. Maybe she'd been too much for her mother to handle.

"It's not your fault, you know. Sometimes it feels like it is, but it isn't." His hand on her cheek moved to her hair, threading through the wild strands that were slightly damp with melted snow. The heat in his eyes burned slowly, like a fire in a hearth.

Kat's body responded, her thighs clenching together and her nipples hardening. From a single hot, tender look, she was melting for this intense, handsome stranger. A shiver racked her, and he chuckled. Did he know how much he was affecting her? He had to, with that pleased look gleaming in his eyes, and his lips twitching in bemusement.

"Let's get you inside so you can warm up and eat your birthday cake."

She came back to herself and realized they'd been standing inside the courtyard, unmoving, just standing so close, breaths mingled and almost whispering as they opened up about their lives.

They walked up to the front of the red brick dormitory, and he followed her up the small set of steps to her door on the first floor. She turned, ready to thank him for walking her home, but he caught the door, preventing it from shutting.

"May I come inside?" He tilted his head toward the door, and she saw he was still carrying the cake.

"I..." she swallowed down the nervous lump in her throat. She wasn't ready to say good night, or goodbye. But she didn't want him thinking she was the sort of girl who slept with someone she just met. He seemed to sense her indecision.

"Just for cake," he said. "You have my gentleman's promise." He used his index finger to draw a cross over his heart.

A gentleman's promise? She remembered the things those girls had said back in the pub. Was he the sort of man to break a promise? Or just a girl's heart?

Take a chance, a little voice whispered inside her head. *He's a risk worth taking, at least tonight.* If she did let him inside, she'd get to spend more time with him.

She didn't want to let him out of her sight, not until she'd figured him out. She'd always loved puzzles, and this strange, sexy man was more of a puzzle than anything she'd ever seen.

"Okay. But just for a few minutes." She let him follow her inside. It was large for a dormitory room, with a tiny kitchen counter against one wall and a small bathroom. Flicking on the one overhead light, she took the bakery box from Tristan and set it on her desk before turning around to face him. She couldn't help but wonder what he'd think of the world she'd built in the few short months she'd lived here.

The walls were a pale, eggshell white, and she'd covered most of them with posters of famous British people. Tristan eyed one above her bed.

"Lord Nelson? Good God, that sure explains your drink tonight at the Pickerel." He burst out laughing. "What is it like to wake up to that each morning?" The rich sound of his amusement warmed her insides all over again, and she started laughing, too.

"My father got it for me as a joke, and I loved it. I thought he deserved a place of honor."

The throaty laugh that escaped his lips was husky this time. "Above a woman's bed is certainly a place of honor." His gaze roved over her full-sized bed, with its dark royal blue and white fleur-de-lis pattern.

Simple and elegant. *Just like him. He'd look so good on my bed.* The thought made her blush.

It was the first time she'd really let herself go there. When she'd dated in high school, she'd never let herself think about sex. It was pointless to build that connection with someone when her father might be transferred to a new location at any time, and they'd have to pack up their lives again. But she wasn't going to be moving for the next three years. Maybe now was the time to give it a chance.

Tristan stripped off his coat and laid it over the back of her desk chair. She had a brief moment to admire his body from behind, the lean lines of his legs, the broad, muscular shoulders outlined by his sweater, before he would notice her staring. The man was gorgeous. Too gorgeous. It was intimidating, yet she didn't want to look away.

She was still staring when he straightened and faced her. Oh, what he could do to her with that body...Tristan was making her feel a little crazy. Okay, really crazy. She wanted to touch him, to put her hands on his chest, feel that heat she remembered from the pub, and kiss him again. God, she wanted to kiss him, and it almost made her hurt with hunger.

"How about we taste that cake?" He grinned almost lazily, as if he'd known she'd been thinking sinful thoughts.

"Uh...right." She dug through her cabinet and found a pair of blue plates, a knife, and two forks. She cut two slices and held one out to him.

He didn't take his plate right away, instead reaching into the bag from the bakery and retrieving the little packet of candles. He nestled one on the top of her slice.

"You don't need to—"

"Of course I do." He produced a small lighter with a silver crest embossed on it and flicked it on, the flame sparking as he put it to the wick of the candle. The crest matched the one engraved on the gold signet ring on his left hand.

Another part of the mystery. What sort of man wore a signet ring? Given what she knew about history, especially English history, she had to wonder if he might be...No that was silly. He couldn't be royalty. She knew enough about the current monarchy to know he wasn't related to Prince William or Prince Harry. Was he titled? A lord? If so, what was he doing studying at Cambridge? It wasn't unusual for nobles to send their children to study at Oxford or Cambridge, but after they'd gotten their undergraduate degree they didn't normally pursue graduate studies. Of course, the simpler explanation was that he was simply wearing the ring as a fashion statement. A lot of British movie stars wore signet rings to give themselves an aura of mystery.

"What's the symbol on your ring?" she asked, nodding at his hand.

A shadow flickered across his eyes, and he glanced away before he replied. "A family heirloom."

That only created a hundred other questions, but she was prevented from asking anything else because he'd successfully lit the candle.

Once the wick caught fire and burned steadily, he pocketed the lighter and took the plate from her hands.

"Now make a wish and blow it out." Tristan's eyes locked with hers, and that enchanting blue-green was now bright with fire. They were so close, only the plate separating them, as he watched her, waiting.

She leaned down, closed her eyes.

I wish... What did she wish for? A funny thought popped into her head, and she felt strange enough to go with it.

I wish to have an adventure. She was tired of reading about them between the pages of old books, she wanted to live one. Standing here with Tristan and kissing him tonight was the start, and she wanted more, so much more. With a puff, she blew out the candle, and smoke curled up from the blackened tip of the wick.

"Happy birthday, Kat," Tristan whispered.

"Thank you." Kat meant for more than just his sweet words. She meant for the cake, for the kiss in the pub, for setting her down a path of living. She flicked her gaze up to his again as she removed the candle from the slice of cake and set it aside on the counter.

A slow smile curved his lips as he handed back her plate and collected his own. Then he walked over to her bed and sat down.

Tristan tasted his cake, and she wished he were tasting her. She wanted to be back in his arms, kissing him. And part of her was curious to know what made him so notorious that women were whispering about him in pubs.

I have to be smart about this. There was no way she could ask him to kiss her again and open that door to more intimacy. Not after he'd made a promise to behave like a gentleman and just eat his cake. But she was torn. Wanting him to stay, wanting more, and being afraid of that desire and where it could lead. After just a short while of being around him, she could see that heartbreaker side to him, the one that would hurt her if she fell for him. He was full of charm, sex appeal, and mystery. There wasn't a woman in the world who wasn't intrigued by that, or seduced by that...

"Mmm...The baker wasn't lying. This cake is sinful." He patted the bedside next to him. "Come sit."

Kat tried to ignore her confusion about Tristan and the way he made her feel. Hesitant, excited, off balance, fascinated. He was too handsome to be in her room and on her bed. And his simple presence on her bed made her mind go to wonderful places. The images he put in her head with just a thought should have scared her. She wanted to do things with him that she'd never thought about before. Like having him push her flat onto her back and pin her wrists on either side of her head while he kissed her, ruthless, seductive, hard, as she wriggled beneath him, desperate for more. His eyes promised that and so much more as he licked his lips and watched her.

She was finally nineteen, but he made her want to be twenty-five, worldly and experienced. Being around Tristan, she wanted to be someone interesting. Which brought her back to a question that plagued her: Was he pretending to be interested, wanting another notch on his bedpost and thinking she'd be an easy target?

Or does he really like me? A nervous flutter stirred in her stomach again.

"Why did you really follow me to the bakery?" she asked.

For a man like him to come after her when the pub had been filled with plenty of pretty college girls, there had to be a reason. She wasn't exactly the type of girl guys flocked after. She was a size twelve, definitely curvy, with brown hair and gray eyes. Not a stunning model or even like the prettier girls she'd seen on campus, those tall leggy British beauties who were similar to his cousin Celia.

Tristan bit into a forkful of cake, sucking chocolate off the prongs.

Kat stared at his mouth, remembering all too well how his lips had felt on hers.

"You've caught my attention, Kat." He set his plate on the table by the bed and folded his arms over his chest.

"Your attention?" She avoided the bed and sat at her desk, where she nibbled on the cake. The flavors were decadent. The zing of the raspberry, the dark, almost erotic taste of the semi-sweet chocolate. *Sinful.*

"Yes." He reached up to stroke his jaw. "Very few things attract my attention. But *you* did." His brows drew together.

What did that mean? Kat had trouble swallowing.

Maybe if she drank something...Kneeling by her fridge, she retrieved a small carton of milk.

"Want something to drink?" she offered.

"Yes. Thank you." He rose from the bed and came up behind her. The warmth of his body seared hers as he reached around her to grab one of her mugs and fill it himself.

A shiver rippled down her spine, and she closed her eyes a brief moment, until he stepped back again. Then she raised her glass to her lips and hastily drank, trying to quench the thirst chocolate always created, and this newer thirst for the man not two feet from her. He was like a drug—one hit and she needed more. To feel that giddy rush when he pinned her against a wall, his hands exploring her curves, his mouth possessing hers...She was supposed to be playing it cool, and not letting him think he could get her into bed, at least not tonight. The fact that this was exactly what she wanted was very...very bad.

✵ 4 ✵

"I find you fascinating," Tristan said. Their faces were so close, his lips a mere breath from hers, and it made her head spin a little with a strange, excited dizziness. His gaze dropped to her lips as his voice softened to a low murmur. "I made a promise tonight, and I won't break it, even it if bloody well kills me."

Kat shivered and when she spoke her voice was husky. "But after tonight?"

With a curve of his lips, Tristan leaned in half an inch closer. "After tonight...I could fuck you here, in this bed, and leave you so sated you'd wouldn't want to get up for days. The things I could do to you to make you purr, make you moan and beg...After being with me, no other man would satisfy you." The tips of their noses brushed as he leaned a tiny bit closer. Every muscle in her body tensed in heady anticipation, and her heart thudded against her ribs so hard it hurt.

Those images his words created, his body on top of hers, his weight trapping her while he owned her in every way...why did it sound so wonderful and frightening all at the same time?

Kat's lips parted, but no words came out at first.

He seemed like a man who, up to now, had gotten everything he ever wanted. She didn't want to be another thing he got simply because he wanted it. She was a woman worth fighting for, and Kat wanted him to earn her. Her father used to say, "A good man will climb to the highest branch for the ripest apple, rather than pluck the low-hanging fruit." She deserved a man who was willing to work for her.

"But not tonight," she replied softly, almost teasing. Her heart pounded at a wild pace and her hands shook as she clenched them together.

As though it were the most natural thing in the world, he slid an arm around her waist, pulling her in to his body. Her hands came up on instinct, settling on his chest, but she didn't push him away.

"Not tonight," he agreed. "But that one kiss at the Pickerel? It was only the beginning." His arm around her waist tightened.

His words, so determined and confident, made her shiver. There was no denying his confidence was appealing, but this was her sex life they were talking about. She had never been the type of girl to just give in to a guy, so why was saying yes so tempting?

I need to put some space between us. When he's too close I can't think.

She pressed her hands against his chest and, after a long moment, Tristan released her. Kat took a few steps back, heart hammering. He didn't come after her, but instead studied her room again, his eyes fixing on the bookshelf near her door. Kat watched him as he approached the books and studied the titles.

"Jules Verne? Are you a fan of his?" He used one long index finger to tug a book out of her shelf. It was a well-worn paperback version of *The Mysterious Island*. One of her favorites.

Her nervousness was momentarily forgotten.

Talking about books was safe. A lot safer than talking about kisses and where they might lead. "My father read them to me when I was a kid. Verne, Burroughs. They're like my comfort food. I read them over and over."

"Which do you like best?" He nodded at her shelf. She couldn't help but smile as she walked over to him and took the book from his hands, flipping through the pages before meeting his gaze again.

"This one is by far my favorite," she said, indicating the book she now held. Even though she'd put space between them a moment ago, she felt safe now, standing here, talking about books. It helped her think clearly, past the hazy desire that filled her whenever he was too close.

Tristan watched her, his captivating eyes darkening with emotions she couldn't quite understand.

"A woman who appreciates classic literature that isn't Austen, Hardy, or one of the other stereotypes of the classic literature world. What a rare find you are. Do you know most women your age haven't even read a book in years? It's all magazines and online gossip sites. Bloody empty-headed creatures, the lot of them." There was something about his words, the way he spoke…it was as though he were frustrated and annoyed.

Kat wondered if Tristan had tried to talk to other women he'd slept with and found them lacking. The idea that she might be different from those women… hope stirred inside her.

"Don't get me wrong. I like Austen and Hardy, but an author's works should move you. I don't want to claim an author is a favorite just because they're considered a classic. Verne's diction, his imagination, his characters—they leap off the page and sweep me away." As she spoke, she gazed fondly at the titles lining the bookshelf. So many wonderful memories, so many stories. All with the power to make her forget the pain she'd had in life, the way her mother had abandoned her, the way her father buried himself in his job. With books, she'd found the solace she needed. The stories didn't change, the characters didn't leave, and she didn't have to leave them behind when she moved. Not like her real life.

But I'm done hiding. Cambridge is home for three years. I can take a risk now.

It was a lot easier to go out and try new things if people like Mark and Lacy were there with her as a safety net. Lacy had taken her clubbing the first night they'd met. Kat had hated the whole experience, but she'd been glad she'd had Lacy to go and try it out with. And Mark had talked her into learning how to punt on the River Cam even though she was convinced she'd never be able to stay on the boat while standing, let alone steer it. But she had, because he'd been there to help her.

It was definitely time to try any- and everything because she had the chance to.

"And you want to be swept away?" Tristan moved, reaching up to trap her between himself and the wall.

Her body jolted at the sudden vulnerable position, every muscle twitching as though she were a live wire. How could he do that to her? Make her body act so crazy with just the simple act of caging her in? His eyes searched hers, his face completely focused on her as he seemed to be waiting for an answer, and she struggled to remember his question.

"Sometimes I do," she admitted, her gaze landing on his lips. They were such soft, kissable lips, but the rest of him was lean, strong, *hard*. She couldn't forget the way it felt to be pressed up against him, his body dominating hers as he kissed her senseless.

He made a low, throaty sound, almost between a

hum and a growl as he leaned down, ever so slowly, and touched his lips to hers.

There was ample time to push him away, but the memory of that first kiss...it was seared into her. Kat had to know if Tristan could make her feel like that again.

It's not seduction, it's just another little harmless kiss...

The soft brush of their mouths was gentle, but heat began to build. The way he licked at her lips, entreating her to open her mouth, was erotic, dangerous. There was nothing sweet about it.

Could a man's kiss feel hotter than sex?

She'd never had sex before, and she couldn't help but wonder if it felt like this with everyone or if it was just Tristan—the all-consuming hunger and the languorous feel of her body as she arched her back, pressing closer to him.

One of his hands gripped the back of her neck as he deepened the kiss. The feel of his tongue playing with hers as his hips rocked forward, pinning her against the wall, sent them both climbing toward something powerful *together* but he was in charge and she liked it, oh how she *liked* it. Everything he did was overpowering, and he worshipped her with his mouth until she was ready to come undone.

There was no ignoring the impressive bulge of his arousal when it pressed into her stomach through her jeans.

A gasp escaped her, but he swallowed her sounds of shock and pleasure. He cupped her ass, lifted her up, and held her trapped between the wall and his body.

"Tristan!" she breathed between his heady kisses. It stunned her that he could hold her up, one-handed, their bodies as close as two people could get with their clothes on.

"You are...quite the most—" he panted against her

mouth, "exquisite creature. All honey and fire..." He stole another deep, lingering kiss. The kind that made her body flush and a quiver of longing fly through her like quicksilver. She didn't want it to ever end, this feeling of rushing wildly toward something immense and wondrous, just within reach—

Tristan let her feet drop to the floor but didn't put any distance between them as he continued to trail kisses from her mouth down to her throat, nipping and sucking at newly sensitive spots that made her whimper. He continued to encroach upon her space, his muscular build and height making her feel small and vulnerable as he kept her caged in his arms.

Kat never had wanted to feel small or vulnerable before but, in that moment with Tristan, it was wonderful. She was a woman, utterly feminine, full of new passion and desire, not a girl with no sexual experience. His kisses had *changed* her. Hating to admit it, she knew he was right. Whatever this was between them, it was explosive.

He caressed the back of his knuckles across her cheek before he stepped away.

"I should go...Wouldn't want to break my promise."

She bit her bottom lip, holding back the words that would make him stay. Kat wasn't ready to take the next step, no matter how much her body screamed for her to keep him here.

"Okay." The word came out breathless and a little shaky. Her entire body was strung out on an edge, craving him, wanting more of what his kisses hinted was to come, but she wasn't ready.

"Happy birthday, darling. I'll see you soon." His eyes held a merry twinkle that softened his intensity, making him more playful.

He slipped out the door, and she shut it behind him, then leaned against it, catching her breath.

Raising a hand to her mouth, she explored her tender lips, swollen from his ravaging kisses.

How strange and wondrous the night had turned out. She'd gotten her wish. Spending tonight with Tristan had been an adventure. Kissing him, the feeling of being in his arms, it wasn't something she'd ever forget.

He'd been so...dominant and assertive, and taken control, as though he'd known it was what she needed.

I shouldn't like that. I know I shouldn't. But I do...

Kat nibbled her lip in frustration. What was wrong with her? She'd never cared this much about any guy before, and had certainly never let one twist her into knots before, either. There was just something about him, and she couldn't get him out of her mind.

It wouldn't be like this tomorrow, when she'd be busy cramming for final exams and shouldn't be thinking about him. But tonight, she could close her eyes and still feel that devilish and delicious brush of Tristan Kingsley's kiss upon her lips. Seductive, mysterious, and all too dangerous because of what his kiss promised.

⁂ 5 ⁂

Tristan walked out of Magdalene College's dorms and waved at the porter. Snow crunched beneath his boots, and he grinned at the flurry of memories from the evening. He'd gone to the pub to meet his favorite cousin, only to have the most tantalizing little creature just grab him and kiss him. Her bold, open responses had lit a fire inside him. He didn't often pursue Americans for even one night of passion, but with Kat he wanted to make an exception. Risking his father's wrath to taste her sweetness was an added incentive he couldn't pass up.

There was no way he'd let a woman like her vanish, not after the kiss they'd shared. There was something about her, the way her eyes had softened into a dreamy look just after he'd stopped kissing her, like a princess born in a garden who'd only ever seen the beauty of blooming flowers. It had been...fascinating, addictive to watch the passion darken her gray eyes to a rich silver.

And it wasn't just her body that intrigued him. This was a woman who talked of fractal snowflakes and kept old Victorian adventure novels as her closest friends. He had sensed how lonely she was when he'd glimpsed the inside of her dorm room. The walls had been covered with portraits of people long dead with no connection to her, beacons of history, but cold, empty companions. She'd only had a few photos of her and a man he guessed was her father, posing awkwardly before various venues. There hadn't been the usual collage of pictures of smiling girls he'd expected to see. His little American was afraid to make friends, to get out and experience things.

One night with me will change that.

And he planned to have that night, show her how hot the fire between them could burn, soon.

When he'd touched her books and asked about her taste in literature, the way her eyes had lit up! It had aroused him. A woman talking about books, of all things, had made him so bloody hard he'd been glad his coat had concealed his condition, at least until he'd pinned her to the wall for another kiss. There was something deeper though, that loneliness in her eyes had called to him, and he'd felt that answering echo from deep within. Despite his close relationship with his cousin Celia and his best friend Carter, he had little in the way of friends. His father had seen to it that his only connections had been other highborn children, and he hadn't liked the company. They were all vain, arrogant, highbrows, just like his father.

A charming innocence clung to her, and when he kissed her, everything inside him seemed to go still and explode at the same time. He wanted to know everything about her. What made her tick, what went on inside that head of hers, and then he wanted to get her beneath him on a bed and take her to places of pure pleasure she'd never dreamed she could go.

The need to possess her in every way possible was so strong, his body vibrated with it. He was Tristan Kingsley, a man who could have any woman he desired for the night, according to Carter, but after meeting Kat, he was convinced that wasn't true. She'd let him kiss her, but she hadn't agreed to climb into his bed. She'd issued him a delightful challenge by not letting him stay the night—she just didn't know it. This was a woman who needed not only her body, but her heart and mind to be seduced as well.

And I'm certainly up to the challenge.

When he reached his Aston Martin, he brushed a gloved hand over the light dusting of snow on the side mirror before he unlocked the car. As he got inside and the engine purred to life, he closed his eyes and rubbed his hands together, attempting to restore some warmth to them.

Unbidden, a sinful memory of how good it felt to have Kat in his arms took hold. She was the perfect size for him, with healthy curves, a short but not too petite frame, hair that begged a man to grasp it and keep her captive during a hard fuck or a slow kiss. It'd been a long time since he'd wanted a woman so badly.

Heat flooded him at the thought of bedding his sweet little Kat. Tristan smiled and started the drive back to his home. He lived outside of the city's main center in a country house his mother owned called Fox Hill. She was currently in residence in London, and he had the good fortune to stay there while he completed his Master's degree. He felt more connected to Fox Hill and Cambridge that he ever had to his father's estate of Pembroke outside of London.

The streets were empty, the wintry weather keeping everyone indoors. There was something about a snowy night with not a soul around. It made him think of that line from a Robert Frost poem, *"The woods are lovely, dark and deep, but I have promises to keep, and miles to go before I sleep."* His headlights cut through the veils of snow as he drove through the tiny streets onto the road that would take him to Fox Hill.

His Bluetooth lit up, catching his attention. He pressed the button to answer the call. "This is Kingsley," he said.

"Tristan." His father's stoic voice came through the car speakers.

Tristan gritted his teeth before replying. "Yes?"

"Your mother informed me that you have agreed to spend the Christmas holidays with her."

His father, the twelfth Earl of Pembroke, was a cold-hearted bastard, and there was no love lost between him and Tristan. They'd never been able to agree upon anything, especially his future.

His parents had separated when he was thirteen, and his life had changed drastically. While they still fought over him on the holidays, he had been able to spend more time with his mother and less with his father.

"Is she telling the truth? I thought perhaps she was attempting to provoke me into another heart episode."

Tristan clenched his teeth to keep from replying with a biting comment. The heart attack his father had suffered six months before hadn't managed to kill him. The earl would likely outlive everyone out of spite, and no amount of preparation to take over the estate on Tristan's part would matter.

"Don't say that about her," Tristan warned. If there was one thing about the old man Tristan couldn't stand, it was his father's poor treatment of his mother.

Ignoring Tristan's outburst, his father continued. "Your place is here. You will be my successor, the thirteenth Earl of Pembroke, and it is imperative that you do your duty. I can't spend all my time chasing after you to come home where you belong. I've been busy in the House with the European Union discussions and don't have time to babysit you. You should be here at home, at my side, or have you forgotten that this is the life you were born into?"

He gripped the steering wheel so hard his hands ached. "Forget? How can I? Ever since I learned to walk and talk, that's all you've ever told me. *My duty.* God forbid I want to have a life of my own."

The biting laugh on the other end of the phone line cut him to the bone. "Your own life? Tristan, you understand nothing. Your life doesn't and will never belong to you. It belongs to your country, to the government, to the people of Britain. You, just like any king or prince, must do your duty."

"I'm not a bloody prince, Father. Even William and Harry have more freedom than I do!" he snapped.

"Freedom is a fickle creature, Tristan." His father's voice was suddenly quieter. "You don't need it as much as you think you do. Once you settle down at the estate, you'll realize that."

A strange, choking despair seemed to fill Tristan's lungs, and he couldn't speak. He had bigger plans, and he wasn't going to let his father trap him into the same unhappy existence that had broken his parents' marriage. A life to live that would never really be his... He knew what his father wanted. No more wild nights in Monte Carlo, no more classes at Cambridge, no more kissing a certain American girl. That would give his father a heart episode for sure.

"Tristan, you are coming here for Christmas, do you understand?" His father's imperial tone was frosted with ill humor and plenty of anger. It was the one emotion he never seemed to have an issue displaying.

"Whatever you say, Father," Tristan said, but it was a flat-out lie. He had no intention of showing up at the estate for Christmas holidays. The old bastard could rot and die for all he cared.

"Good." His father disconnected the call.

Tristan turned his car into the short, curved driveway and parked it in front of the main entrance. The only other people in residence were a small staff, consisting of a cook, a maid, a butler, and Tristan's best friend Carter Martin.

Carter was the son of John Martin, the current steward of the Kingsley estate. Tristan and Carter had grown up together, playing in secret when Tristan's father wasn't around. The old man was bloody strict about knowing one's place in society. The future Earl of Pembroke could not be friends with a steward's son. But Tristan rarely obeyed his father's dictates, which meant that he and Carter had been inseparable since they'd been old enough to toddle about the Kingsley gardens.

Fox Hill was quaint in comparison to his father's home, but it was fairly large as cottages went, with six bedrooms, a library, two drawing rooms, one study, a kitchen, and a dining room.

The electric lamps in their gilded sconces were dim as Tristan entered the front hall, but he could see the delicate gold arms of the grandfather clock at the foot of the stairs, showing that it was half past midnight. Everything in the house had that old English feel to it, unsurprising given that the house itself was over a hundred years old. His mother had kept the property updated but the look was relatively unchanged.

His mother, Elizabeth, was an only child and had married well in hopes of pleasing her parents. As the daughter of a viscount, her marriage to an earl had been one well above her station and quite an accomplishment. But his father saw her social climb differently; as he had once put it, "I was young and let beauty foolishly lead my decisions." He failed to value Elizabeth and didn't even care to acquire her "quaint little country home," which had suited his mother just fine. She'd kept the cottage outside of their marriage arrangements, and when the time had come for Tristan to go back to university for his Master's degree, he'd asked his mother if he and Carter could stay there. They both attended Cambridge, and the cottage was a short drive away.

"You're back late." Carter stood in the doorway leading to the library, a grin on his lips. "Up to trouble again?"

Tristan smiled. He and Carter were the same age, though Carter was fair where Tristan was dark, and his eyes gray where Tristan's were blue-green. Celia often called them her pair of angels, one fair and good, the other dark and fallen. Accurate to some degree. Carter was a good man and one of Tristan's confidantes. He often reined in Tristan's reckless impulses. However, Carter was no angel himself.

"How was Celia?" Carter asked.

Tristan flashed him a smirk. "Well, I suppose."

"You suppose? Does that mean you didn't see her?" Carter pushed away from the door frame he'd been leaning against. "Weren't you having drinks with her tonight?"

"I did see her," Tristan admitted. "But I had to leave before I could really talk to her."

"What on earth for?" Carter's puzzlement only made Tristan want to laugh.

"Because I had to chase down a most fascinating little creature instead."

Carter rolled his eyes. "You and your women. What's this one like?"

My women. Tristan shrugged. He'd slept with his fair share of them, but never anything serious. Women were fun distractions.

Kat, though...His blood heated at the mere

thought of her. She'd captivated him tonight at the Pickerel, and he'd chased after her.

He'd finally caught up to her and seen her through the ice-frosted windows of the bakery...her hair wild and free about her shoulders, the classically beautiful features of her face temporarily caught in an expression of hunger and desire as she'd eyed the cakes. He'd wanted to take her to bed then and there, to make her look at *him* with that expression of need.

"Let's just say, this particular woman is different."

"Different, eh?" Carter laughed. "Well, I hope Celia wasn't too upset."

Tristan slipped out of his coat and raised an eyebrow at his friend. "Not terribly. We're having lunch tomorrow, if you'd like to join us." He waited to see if Carter would rise to the challenge. For as long as Celia had been in their lives, Carter had been in love with her. Not that he would ever admit to it.

"Lunch tomorrow?" Carter mused.

"Yes. I know she'd love to see you." Tristan hung his coat in the closet by the door. Mr. Whitney, the butler, was usually asleep after ten. Tristan and Carter had grown accustomed to taking care of themselves in the evening.

"Perhaps I shall. Are you going up?"

Tristan nodded. "It's been a long day, and I have much to do tomorrow."

"Do you ,now?" Carter followed, a hint of teasing in his voice.

"I do. You ought to worry about what you'll wear when you see Celia." Tristan left his friend with that parting shot as he reached his bedroom.

With a sigh, he leaned against the door once he was inside and tilted his head back. As tired as he was, he wouldn't sleep well, not when he knew he would dream about *her*.

She will be mine. She just doesn't know it yet.

❧ 6 ❧

K at settled into a corner of Pepys Library, taking advantage of the quiet reading rooms. With its many windows framed by buttery gold brocade curtains and rich blue carpets, the atmosphere felt cheery even during the winter months.

Tall, dark wooden bookshelves lined the wall opposite the row of windows. Reading desks and display cases alternated through the middle of the room. The library had originally belonged to Samuel Pepys, who had served as secretary to the admiralty for many years. He'd contributed a unique collection of three thousand books and manuscripts to Magdalene College.

Everything was preserved the way Pepys had left it, right down to the glazed bookcases that he'd had made by the dockyard joiners over the years.

She smiled as she studied the room. So full of history. *This* was what made her love Cambridge. When her father had taken the job in London and asked if she wanted to attend the university over here, she'd jumped at the chance. Every few weekends, she'd catch a bus back to London to see her father, but hadn't done so recently. With exams drawing near, she needed to stay focused. Which was hard, given how the previous night had ended—Tristan Kingsley pinning her to the wall and kissing her like...

A shiver moved through her, and she tried to shake off the wave of desire that accompanied it. What had happened between them had been a one-night experience, nothing more. It'd been an explosive introduction to a passion she didn't know she had. Kissing him had been like waking up from a strange dream where everything had been dull, quiet, and muted.

Tristan had burst into her life like a supernova. Overnight he'd given her a taste of sensuality. In the space of a few kisses, he had shown her that some adventures weren't buried between the pages of her books, but could be experienced in the arms of a dark, handsome stranger on a snowy night.

A sigh of regret escaped her as she stared out of the library windows. The odds of seeing Tristan again were slim. He was a student here, but not at her college. And it was unlikely that he'd try to find her, not when there were plenty of other girls interested in him, like the ones at the Pickerel Inn. He could have his choice, and she highly doubted that, after her refusal to let him stay the night, he'd go after her again.

It was almost laughable.

They were too different, like birds and fish, their worlds infinitely separate. Yet when they'd talked, everything seemed to click and make sense. He seemed to understand her obsession with classic novels, and he liked that she knew strange things like what fractals were. Just as she liked how he responded intelligently when she talked to him, and how he stared at her with such an intensity that she felt he was actually listening to what she was saying. But it was more than that. He seemed to see straight into the heart of her, somehow. They were connected by the need to think about the world on a deeper level than other people and appreciate the beauty of things, even sad things. Anyone could have common interests and discuss books, but with Tristan it was different; he understood her, the way she viewed the world. No one else seemed to understand her the way he did, and she had the feeling that she understood him in the same way, by the way he talked about things. *Like Butterflies and stained glass.* Anyone else might have laughed at their conversation in the pub, but it had been one of the deepest, frankest discussions she'd ever had with anyone. Tristan had made it easy to open up. Of course, it was also impossible to ignore how irresistible he was. The man had everything a woman could want: looks, brains, and that sheer power of true animal magnetism.

Kat wouldn't even start on his drugging kisses... That didn't need an explanation. She'd wanted so badly for him to stay the night, even though it went against all her instincts to keep herself protected from him, not just physically but emotionally. Kat didn't think for a moment he would hurt her, but she could fall for a guy like him, and when you fell, it could break you. She'd seen her father live with a broken heart. Never dating, never going out, never living. She didn't want that to happen to her.

I want to live... That little voice in the back of her head just wouldn't shut up. *I'm already acting like I've had my heart broken. Would it be so bad to take a risk?*

Her exams were too important, and she couldn't let her focus drift to thoughts of Tristan. Especially not how wonderful it felt to have his body wrapped around hers, his hands exploring places that still tingled with the memory of his touch. Her entire body had threatened to come apart at the seams when his lips and hands traced patterns on her skin.

"How was last night?" Lacy appeared out of

nowhere, breaking into Kat's naughty thoughts of Tristan.

"What do you mean? I spent last night with you."

Lacy scoffed as she grabbed one of the extra chairs nearby and dragged it across the floor to put it next to Kat. She plopped down into the seat and dropped her backpack to the floor.

"Oh no, you are *not* getting out of this." Lacy shook a finger at her. "Mark and I saw Mr. Hotness ditch his girlfriend and leave the bar to go after you. We were worried, so we followed him. We saw him meet up with you at the bakery and walk you back to the dorms. So...what happened after that?" She brushed her blonde hair out of her eyes and assumed an attentive pose, which, for someone like Lacy, who seemed to be in constant motion, looked a little funny.

Obviously, Kat wouldn't escape Lacy's interrogation. She set her textbook and notebook aside.

"So...he walked me home." *And rocked my world.*

"Uh-huh. And then what?" Lacy propped her chin in her hands, waiting expectantly.

Kat would have to edit some of the night's events or her friend would demand to know everything that'd happened. What she and Tristan had shared was a secret she wanted to keep. Talking about it might make it disappear or fade away. A silly thought, but it was how she felt.

"He came to my room, and we shared some chocolate cake."

"And hot sweaty sex?" Lacy added with a cheeky grin.

"No!" Kat laughed and tossed a pen at her friend.

"No hot sweaty sex?" Lacy sighed in disappointment. "Don't tell me you weren't tempted. If Mark and I weren't together, I'd climb that man like a tree."

"Lacy!" Kat gasped, torn between horror and

amusement. Thank God no one else was in this part of the library. She and Lacy could get kicked out for being too much of a distraction.

Her friend shrugged. "What? A girl can't own up to desire? I think it's healthy."

Kat rubbed her eyes, an exasperated laugh escaping her. "You know I'm not like that."

"Oh, I know." Lacy toyed with the pen, tapping it on the polished surface of the reading table.

"So, who is 'Mr. Sexy as Hell'?" Lacy asked. "I swear, it's strange, but I feel like I've seen him somewhere before. Maybe on campus?" She pursed her lips.

"Tristan Kingsley."

"Kingsley?" Lacy asked. "I know that name...Let's see what Google can tell us about him." She pulled out her tablet and typed away on the screen for a few seconds, then smacked it down on the table. "Oh... he's...bloody hell. Take a look." She spun the device toward Kat, who saw a webpage for a magazine.

"*Monarch Magazine*?" Kat leaned forward and stared at the website.

"It focuses on the royals here in England and around the world. My mum's a huge fan. She reads all the articles and keeps me updated. I thought your Mr. Sexy-as-Hell looked familiar." She pointed to the article.

"What's it say?" Kat sat up in her chair and leaned closer to Lacy.

"It's him, your mystery man. Tristan Kingsley. He's the future Earl of Pembroke."

There on the top part of article was a picture of Tristan, her Tristan, in an expensive suit, lounging against the doorjamb of the grand entrance to a huge manor house that looked to be in the country outside of London. The article was titled "Tristan Kingsley— The Life of a British Playboy."

Kat slowly scrolled down the page of *Monarch*'s article, reading the captions and staring at the photos. There was one of Tristan in a tweed hunting outfit, a rifle loose on one arm as he stood at the edge of a field, an older man stood next him holding a string with a pair of dead pheasants hanging from it. The next photo was of Tristan in slacks and a sweater in a beautiful billiard room, bent over, cue in hand as he aimed for the brightly colored balls. His dark hair fell across his eyes and the debonair look of him was all too reminiscent of how seductive he could be.

The next page displayed a red-and-gold-colored coat of arms. It was the crest she'd seen on his silver lighter and the signet ring he wore. So he hadn't been lying when he'd called it a family heirloom. Beneath the coat of arms was a lengthy description of the earldom's history. Twelve names dating back several hundred years showed the lineage. The most recent showed Edward Kingsley as the current earl. A family tree outlined the latest descendants. Elizabeth Harlow had married Edward Kingsley and given birth to Tristan Kingsley.

"Heir to the earldom of Pembroke?" Was this real? She'd been kissing a man who was a peer of the realm of England? First in line for the title of "Earl of Pembroke"?

There was no way she'd spent last night making out with a future earl. *No way*. It just didn't seem logical that he'd be here at Cambridge. Didn't future earls have estates to run or something? What was he doing here? The British aristocracy, even in this day and age, tended to stay with their own kind. They didn't date American girls. They might sleep with them quietly on the sly, but she hadn't heard of them actually dating anyone outside their own social sphere.

"He's getting a Master's in business. Why would

he need that if he's going to inherit money, land, and a title?" Kat studied the photos on the *Monarch* website again. They were stunning, but had nothing on the flesh-and-blood man.

Her friend shrugged. "Well, running an estate is pretty intense. It's all about business, so it makes sense for him to get a business degree."

Lacy had a point. "Well, if he's taking business classes, I probably won't run into him."

"Maybe not, but you have to stay away from him if you happen to see him."

"I agree. But you were all for climbing him like a tree two seconds ago."

Lacy shifted in her chair and brushed her hair back from her face. Only then did she meet Kat's eyes.

"He—what's that thing you Americans say?—"gets around"? Besides, a man like him will be in the spotlight all his life, especially once he takes his title. He's from one of the oldest families in England, and they don't often marry outside their own kind. If I remember correctly, he's supposed to marry a viscount's daughter. Funny, I never listened to Mum before when she droned on about all this stuff, but now it's coming back to me."

A man who gets around? Those girls from the pub were right about him.

And one who would end up close to being royalty in a few years? That was definitely the last thing she needed. Someone like him, his life always under a spotlight, and society scrutinizing his every move...If she was with him, she'd be a part of that life. It wasn't something she wanted, to expose herself like that. What if she let her barriers down and he got inside her heart? When they broke up, it would be so public. The thought made her shudder.

We never even had a chance to figure out what it might have been like to be together.

That realization left a burn inside her. She rubbed her chest and glanced away, hating that for some silly reason her eyes stung. She was not going to get upset about Tristan. Not when they didn't know each other at all.

Trying to hide her pain, Kat laughed, but the sound was hollow. "Thank God, I'm too young to date anyone seriously. Besides, he's not my type."

"Tall, dark, and sexy is *every* woman's type," Lacy said, grinning again. "So he's out for real, but at least we can fantasize about him." She picked up her backpack.

"He's too intense for me," Kat admitted.

"'Intense'? What happened? And don't think about not telling me everything, because if you don't, I won't tell you what I heard when I was in your favorite bookstore."

"G. David?" The place was Kat's private refuge from the world. They sold all sorts of used books, including rare and antiquarian tomes. She'd spent many an afternoon there sighing over the more expensive editions.

"Yes. You talk, then I will," Lacy said.

There was nothing like friendship blackmail to make her talk, and Lacy had it down to an art form. Kat would *have* to tell her about the kiss.

"Okay, fine. When Tristan came over, he kissed me again after we had cake."

"And..." Lacy waved for her to continue.

Kat hesitated, but only for a second. "It was crazy intense." The memory of that scorching moment, the way he'd touched her, inside and out, with his erotic kisses. He'd overwhelmed her senses and taken her for a ride that had left her breathless and aching in dark, secret places.

Her friend scooted closer. "Like, how intense?"

"Lacy," Kat said, groaning. "I'm not telling you anything else. It was intense. That's all you're going to get."

"Hmm. Well, it's nice to see you having some fun, Kat. You are way too serious, you know. Burying yourself in books is not the way to spend your life."

"I know, I know." She sighed. She needed to stick to "Operation Adventure." Just because her first foray into the world of living on the edge had ended with her discovering Tristan's sordid romantic and elitist family history, it didn't mean she couldn't keep trying to have fun in other ways. Ways that didn't involve a certain British bad boy. But she wasn't going to let Lacy distract her from her need to hear about G. David. Books would always be a huge part of her life, even if she was out seeking some adventures. They were friends she could take with her whenever she and her father moved. Sure, she'd kept in touch online with a few girlfriends from high school, and Ben occasionally e-mailed or texted, but it wasn't the same as being able to see them in person. It was easy to grow apart from people when you moved away.

I hate good-byes.

But coming here for school meant she was guaranteed three years in the same place. Mark and Lacy were her first real friends in a long time because Kat finally knew for sure that things in her life wouldn't suddenly change.

"Okay, I told you about last night, so what about G. David?"

Leaning close, a conspiratorial twinkle in her eyes, Lacy spoke. "They apparently had someone call in this morning and ask to buy that first edition of *The Mysterious Island* you were staring at last week."

Kat's heart fluttered. She'd never be able to afford

it, but she hadn't been able to resist wanting it. "How'd you find out about it?"

"I overheard one of the store clerks confirming the order while I was buying some Terry Brooks novels."

Kat almost smiled, but then something clicked. An image of Tristan holding on to the worn paperback from her shelf. The way he'd looked at the book, then at her, as though sorting out a puzzle. *No. It couldn't be...*But it was the only conclusion that made sense. He'd seen her book last night and then today he'd gone to G. David and bought the first edition. Did he intend to give it to her? She couldn't see any other reason for him to do that, since he hadn't mentioned that he was a Jules Verne fan.

Kat glanced at her watch. She had about half an hour before her next class, which was just enough time for her to visit the bookshop. She grabbed her books and shoved them into her bag. "I want to see it again before the buyer picks it up."

Lacy followed as they exited the library. The courtyard was covered with snow now, but in the warmer months, the white stone library was a rich contrast against the green grass. There was so much that she loved about Cambridge: the town, the university, the people. It felt more like home than anywhere she'd lived before. Like going to school in a fairy-tale village with castles on every corner.

"If you're going all the way to G. David, I'll catch you later for dinner. Text me, okay?" Lacy called out as they parted ways.

"Bye!" Kat waved but she was already walking, with one thing on her mind. Well, maybe two things, the book and one sexy-as-hell, off-limits, future earl. *Damn.*

G. David was every book lover's dream. It was the epitome of the antiquarian book collector's world, and was tucked away on 16 St. Edward's Passage. The shop's wood storefront was painted blue, making it stand out from the stores around it, like a welcoming little cottage. The name "G. David" had appeared in white, creating a sharp contrast against the blue wood and white brick of the storefront of the building.

Much of the shop was full of the standard sort of used books. Kat meandered through the aisles, her shoulders brushing against the thickly stacked shelves containing hundreds of musty- smelling paperbacks. Some of the pages were yellowed with age and their covers faded. Unable to resist, she trailed a fingertip over their sun-warmed spines, idly reading the titles. A thousand stories hummed from the pages, whispering to her of heroes long gone, and tales of love that spanned centuries.

I could spend my life wandering through this shop, glimpsing worlds through the windows of these books.

She couldn't help but smile as she remembered telling Tristan about Jules Verne and why she liked his stories. The fantastical adventures were addictive, almost as much as kissing him.

She jerked to a halt and shook her head a little, trying to clear it.

Stop thinking about him. The way he smelled of winter and spice, how his warm breath fanned over her face as he panted to regain his breath, and how that had sent shivers of excitement through her.

Glancing about, she looked for the sign pointing to the rare-book room. Once there, she paused in the doorway. Rows of gilded spines glinted beneath the soft lights overhead. Each one seemed to whisper secrets from the stories they held. Bookstores were holy to Kat. They offered adventure and the truth of the human soul, both dark and light.

Goose bumps covered her arms as she touched the spines nearest her, tracing the gilt letters of the titles. Some of the sturdier editions weren't protected by glass casing. The musty scent that clung to the air brought back old memories of her father's library. Her mother hadn't been one for reading. It was her father's lap she'd climbed onto for a story. As she'd gotten a little older, he'd perched on the edge of her bed and read her tales until her eyes had drifted shut and she'd slipped into dreams filled with dragons, warriors, and magic.

Homesickness swamped her, and her throat constricted. She hadn't thought of those days in a long time. The days before she and her father had become nomads. He couldn't bear to stay in one place too long, as the sense of missing something grew stronger over time. Her father used to come into the kitchen and pause, stare at the stove, then, with a sigh, reach for a pot to make dinner.

Cooking had been the one thing her mother had enjoyed. Before she'd left, the stove had always had something good-smelling on the cooktop. After the divorce, the house seemed to be gripped with a gaping void. An emptiness tempered by a quiet sense of grief was embedded in the very brick and wood of the house itself.

Her mother was still very much alive somewhere far away from them, and her leaving had felt like a death, in a way. It was hard to explain, but the pain Kat felt when she thought about her mother was still fresh.

"Hello, can I help you find anything in particular?" A female clerk's voice jerked Kat out of her thoughts. The woman stood at the opposite end of the room, by a narrow wooden door labeled "storage." In her late forties, she had a pair of glasses perched on her nose and a hint of gray in her hair.

She gently dusted the tops of books with a flat paintbrush as she slowly made her way down the nearest shelf toward Kat. It was a sight Kat was used to in old bookstores. Paintbrushes were an ideal dusting tool for books.

"Actually—" Kat shifted her backpack and took a step into the rare book room. "I heard you have a buyer for the first edition of *The Mysterious Island* by Jules Verne. I was wondering if I could look at it before the buyer picked it up. I'm a huge fan, but couldn't afford the edition."

The clerk's eyes lit up. "A Verne fan! We don't see too many of those these days. I'd be happy to let you take a peek at it." The woman winked. "Come, let's get it out."

Each of the books inside the rare-edition glass cabinet had a strip of white paper with a name scrawled in black ink tucked inside its front cover. The lucky owners, Kat guessed.

"Here we are." The woman crooked one index finger onto the top part of the spine and tugged gently so it slid free of its neighbors.

"This is part one. *Dropped from the Clouds*. At the buyer's request we're locating the second and third parts, *The Abandoned* and *The Secret of the Island*." The clerk held out the red leather book.

Kat took it, holding it with reverence. Dark gold letters displayed the title on the cover. Beneath was a gold etching of a hot-air balloon drifting over a calm ocean as though ready to crash into the sea. Someone lucky was going to be taking this home. A pang of envy shot through her, making her feel guilty.

There was something magical about old books. The detail and artistry that went into their creation, with their gilded edges, engraved illustrations, and eye-catching covers, made each of them a treasure. In today's world, there was so much less magic, less wonder in the small things, like the beauty of books. It made her old-fashioned, yet she couldn't help but appreciate the book for what it was, an icon of an era lost forever.

"Lovely, isn't it?"

She nodded, carefully opening the book, studying the title page as she spoke. "How much is the buyer paying for it?" The number was going to make her cringe, but she couldn't resist asking.

"About £1,000.00. He was most insistent we find the others, as well."

Doing the math in her head, Kat winced. That was more than $1,500 dollars for one book. With great reluctance, she returned *Dropped from the Clouds* into the clerk's hands.

"Anything else catch your fancy?" the clerk asked.

Kat shook her head. Her class, European History 1600 to 1800, started in half an hour, which left her no time to browse.

"Do you mind if I asked who bought *Dropped from the Clouds?*" she asked the clerk.

The woman nudged her glasses up her nose an inch, hesitating to speak, as though she was considering if she ought to respect the buyer's privacy.

"I have a friend, a man named Tristan Kingsley. I thought perhaps he might be the one who bought it," Kat clarified. Tristan had no reason to buy it. Still... his flashing blue-green eyes crossed her mind, teasing her with memories of the previous night. She knew it was him. It wasn't a coincidence that the first edition, which had been at G. David's for a year, was being bought the day after Tristan had stood in her bedroom and looked at her battered, well-loved copy.

"Er...well, I'm not permitted to disclose our client's information, but I can say that if it was your friend, he has excellent taste." The clerk gave her a small but knowing smile.

Oh, wow. He'd really done it. The question now was, why? What would he do with a first edition of

Jules Verne, other than give it to her? She couldn't accept a gift like that, it was way too expensive. And she couldn't help but wonder what his reason for buying it for her was. Did he always buy things for the women he claimed he was interested in? Did he expect her to sleep with him after getting a gift like that? It was all too confusing. She didn't know what the protocol was for a girl to do when getting a gift like that. As she headed to class, she struggled to come up with a plan.

Nothing could take that sexy Brit out of her head. And that was a bad sign, since she knew she shouldn't see him again. But what would she do when he gave her the Jules Verne book? Shove him out the door and tell him good-bye when she really just wanted to drag him into her dorm room again? Yeah...she knew without a doubt that if he showed up in her life again, they'd end up in trouble because he would kiss her and if he kissed her it would lead to so much more...

7

"You have that funny look on your face again." Celia laughed softly and nudged Tristan's leg under the table with her high-heeled black boot.

For the last ten minutes, he'd been watching the door of a bookshop, waiting, holding his breath. Kat was inside. It had been sheer luck that he'd convinced Celia to meet him at the little café across the street, because he intended to pick up the book he'd ordered for Kat from G. David's.

They'd only just taken their seats in front of the window when an all-too-familiar, tantalizing figure trudged through the snow to the store across the street.

His Kat. Well...she would be his soon enough.

"Tristan, what is the matter with you? Is everything all right? I've never seen you so distracted. First last night, now this morning. If I didn't know you better, I'd think you were trying to placate me by agreeing to have lunch." Celia frowned when he glanced her way. She always worried about him, but that was part of who she was. While she was beautiful, fashionable, and independent, she had a softer, more nurturing side to her that many daughters of

73

the peerage lacked. Last night, when he'd called off their drinks, she'd let him go, but only if he agreed to meet up today so she could get to see him.

They were first cousins—her mother was Tristan's father's younger sister—but they had grown up together as close as siblings. Tristan had come to appreciate her friendship over the years, and how he could talk to her about everything—well, almost everything. Carter was the one exception. Celia was in love with Carter and couldn't have him because her father would never allow it.

She'd always looked to Carter with those adoring hazel eyes, in a way that sometimes made Tristan jealous. Not because he wanted Celia, but because he longed for a woman of his own to look at him like that. As though he'd hung the moon and captured a string of stars for a necklace. He'd been with plenty of women, all of whom had looked at him like the social stepping-stone he was. Tristan loathed it. As much as he loved the things that his position in society provided, he wanted people to care about who he was as person, not his family's lineage.

"Don't ignore me, cousin," Celia chided, her eyes narrowed. "Out with it. You're distracted by something, and I want to know what it is."

"Are you free next week?" Rather than answer her question, he changed the subject.

"Free for?" She'd make a good countess, or a duchess, if she ever married that high. Knowing her parents, he realized, she'd have to, because they would pressure her to pick a man of their choosing.

"Carter and I were thinking of having an end-of-semester-exams party next weekend. Would you like to help host?"

Celia's face lit up. "I do so love a party." Her excitement quickly morphed into curiosity. "Whenever you say 'you and Carter' it always ends up being only you who did the planning. Does poor Carter know you've roped him into this?"

Tristan shrugged. "Carter will be happy to be involved, especially if you're there." He let the teasing hint drop and took a sip of his hot tea, watching her over the rim of his cup, expecting her to react to his playful hint. But she didn't take the bait, clever Celia, and she composed herself like a queen before replying.

"So, a party next weekend. At Fox Hill, I assume?"

"Yes." His eyes drifted back on the bookshop door as it opened and Kat walked out. Her long hair was slightly curled at the ends, which gave the lustrous locks an enticing bounce. Tristan ached to wrap his fingers in the strands and tug lightly as he kissed her.

The fantasy of possessing her, owning her completely in his bed, was driving him mad. If he played his cards right, he wouldn't have long to wait.

"And you want me to act as hostess for this party?" Celia scooted back in her chair to allow their waiter to set down two bowls of hot soup.

Steam curled up in thick tendrils as Tristan swirled his spoon in his bowl. He wanted nothing more than to eat a burger with brown sauce, but the café didn't have anything like that on the menu. But this was the only place located near G. David's bookshop where he could meet his cousin.

"I'd like you and Carter to help me extend some invitations. You still have connections at Magdalene College, don't you?" It had been Celia's college when she'd attended Cambridge as an undergraduate a few years before.

"Yes, why? You want me to invite the entire college?"

He knew she was joking. Shaking his head, he

continued. "I want you to invite a woman named Katherine Roberts and anyone she's friends with."

His cousin's eyes gleamed like topaz gemstones. "Ah...the truth comes out. So all of this is for a woman? I suspect you think she won't come unless her friends do. Don't tell me you're getting soft, Tristan. Unable to seduce an undergraduate?"

His cousin's teasing bruised his ego, and he winced.

"I'm taking care with this one. She's not like the others." It was no secret that his past relationships had been numerous and easy. Those girls hadn't needed any convincing to climb into bed with him. But he didn't just want to take Kat to bed, he wanted to spend time with her in whatever way he could manage.

"You taking care? What makes this one so special that you don't just sleep with her and toss her to the side like the others?"

Her words dug deep like barbs, even more so because he knew what she said was true. It made him feel like a cad. "Feeling ruthless today, are we?" He turned one of his most charming grins on her.

She giggled against the rim of her teacup. "Perhaps a tad. So who is this Katherine Roberts?"

Tristan had no interest in sharing details on Kat, not with Celia. She was too nosy. The last thing he needed was his cousin inserting herself into his affairs.

"She is an interest of mine. You need know nothing else."

Rather than grow cross with him as she often did when he didn't tell her what she wanted to know, Celia clapped her hands. "Oh, this is famous! Whoever she is, she must be quite a woman to have you tied in knots."

"She is quite a woman. One I can't seem to figure

out. Now, you'll see to getting her invited? Drop on by Fox Hill in the next day or two for dinner so we can plan the party. I want it to be perfect."

"Perfection. That I can do." Celia was almost humming.

"Good. Finish your lunch. I need to collect something at G. David's before my next class, and I should like your opinion."

It was time to begin his seduction of Kat. He wouldn't let up, not until she lowered those barriers and gave in to the passion he'd glimpsed the night before.

I will win her.

He smiled, as his gaze drifted back to the cheery shop entrance of G. David's bookstore.

Books were the key to Kat's heart, and Tristan was going to find his way in. At any cost.

◌◌◌

KAT LAY ACROSS HER BED, EYES HALF-CLOSED AS SHE tried to read her textbook. The same sentences kept blurring together over and over. Not a good sign. Exams were two weeks away and there was so much cramming to do. Except for classes, she'd spent the last seventy-two hours holed up in her room.

Lacy had stopped by twice, attempting to entice her out, but Kat couldn't spare the time, not when a mountain of reading loomed on her desk. The books were stacked more than a foot high, teetering, mocking how she felt about her studying. Classes had proved to be quite a challenge, and although she liked that most days, around exams she definitely didn't.

Blinking, she turned a page, then gave in and rested her cheek against the cool, crisp paper of the book. Maybe just a little nap. It was only eight p.m.

She could doze for half an hour and then study some more.

A sudden knock at her door made her jump. The world spun a little as she roused from that hazy place between sleep and wakefulness.

"Who is it?" Kat called and rubbed her eyes.

The knock sounded again.

Kat stumbled to the door and flung it open, expecting to see her friend.

"Lacy, what are you—" Her words died on her lips as she stared up into the blue-green eyes of Tristan Kingsley.

"Kat." He said her nickname with such seductive decadence that she shivered.

"What are you doing here?" she blurted.

He held up a large paper bag and a box wrapped in baby blue paper with a black bow.

"Dinner and a little something for you. I didn't want to take the chance of trusting the store to deliver this," he said, indicating the box. The warmth in his smile was infectious.

Kat had made a promise to forget him, yet here he was, making her grin. Still...she had to study.

"Tristan, you can't just—"

He ignored her. Using his body, Tristan gently shouldered open the door and walked past her. He eyed her desk, which was covered in an insane collection of papers and research books populated by occasional Post-it notes or pens. Then, with a shrug, he walked over to her kitchen area and set the bag of food and the gift down.

"Hey—" she said, trying to stop him from unpacking the bag.

He turned to look at her, his slow, raking gaze followed by a wicked smile that flushed her clear down to her toes. She wore jeans, a sweater, and fluffy warm socks. Not dressed to impress, but that didn't stop him from staring with open appreciation. Suddenly aware of herself in a way she hadn't been moments before, she crossed her arms and bit her bottom lip.

"Sit, I'll prepare the food. You need to eat well in order to pass your exams, don't you?" He moved to her cabinets and retrieved the silverware.

Stunned into silence, Kat plopped down on the edge of her bed and watched him.

Tristan removed his long black coat and dropped it over her desk chair.

How was it that he could own the room with such a simple action as flinging his coat over a chair?

He wore a black turtleneck and he pushed the sleeves up to his elbows, revealing toned, muscled forearms.

Kat's mouth watered as she pictured herself kissing that light-golden skin. Damn, the man was beautiful. Why did he have to be so sexy? It made it that much harder to focus.

The dark charcoal slacks he wore were snug on his ass, showing off his hips, butt, and thighs. It was quite a sight to watch as he searched for plates. Her body responded with a little clench inside and a flare of heat.

"I take it you've been busy studying for exams and haven't done much else today?" he asked as he put pasta on the dishes. The little black logo emblazoned on the bag was a familiar one. It was one of those fancy, white tablecloth-type restaurants with an expensive wine list. She'd strolled by that Italian place with Lacy more than once, inhaling the scents and wishing they had time to go inside.

The food was still hot enough that steam wafted up from the plate he gave her. Tantalizing aromas of basil mixed with garlic and rosemary teased her nose, and she smiled at the heavenly scent. Tristan pulled a bottle of wine from one of the bags and poured two glasses. He handed her one before seating himself at her desk.

"Tristan," she finally got his name out. "What are you doing here?"

He looked up from his meal. The man possessed an air of entitlement, as though sharing dinner with her was something he had expected would happen. It was irritating but also part of what made him fascinating. He exuded a sense of elegant refinement, too, which, given what she knew about him being the future Earl of Pembroke, made perfect sense.

"I should think that was obvious after last night."

"*Why* are you here?" She still couldn't quite believe that he had come to her room with dinner. With any other guy it might have seemed normal, but this was Tristan Kingsley, a well-known womanizer and a member of the British peerage.

He set his plate down, and walked toward her, holding his glass of wine. He took a long sip, watching her as he did so, and said, "I'm interested in you."

A flutter of nerves filled her chest at his words, but she fought to stay calm. He couldn't know how much he affected her, not if she wanted to stay in control of the situation.

"You mean you're here to try and seduce me." She crossed her arms, silently daring him to deny it.

"Exactly. Starting with the seduction of your mouth by feeding you some excellent local cuisine. And you won't turn me down." He swirled his wineglass as though it were full of warm brandy and looked down at her. His patient stare felt like a challenge, and she felt her body surging with energy, with excitement, to meet it. She rose from the bed, needing to be as close to eye level with him as she could to even the playing field of this new and thrilling game.

"I won't?" She arched one brow. He seriously thought she'd go along with whatever he suggested? It had to be because no one in his life had ever said no to him. Kat was tempted to be the first.

The corner of his mouth twitched in a ghost of a near-smile. "No. You won't. Because you're curious. You can't get me out of your head. Did you dream about me last night?"

How did he know? Those vivid, Technicolor dreams had left her sweaty, aching, and wet. Waking up without him had made her practically scream with frustration.

Raising her chin, she shook her head. "No." She didn't usually lie, but there was no way she was going to admit the truth to him.

With a little chuckle, he took a step toward her and whispered in her ear. "You *did*. I can't help but wonder if they were as good as my dreams about you." He was close enough that she felt his body heat. Then he reached out, one hand resting on her hip, the touch light but strangely possessive. "I had you beneath me for hours. I kissed every inch of you, all those little valleys and hollows of your curves. Lost myself between your thighs and tasted you as you exploded on my tongue..."

Holy fucking hell...

Kat couldn't breathe. He was talking about going down on her? Blood rushed to her face, and she knew with dreaded certainty she was showing him just how much his words were affecting her.

"I—I'm not interested." Another lie.

His lips twitched. "You are. You're blushing, by the way. I'm sure you know that. And your thighs are clenching together. Is that because you're wishing I was between them right now?" His fingertips on her hip stroked slowly upward to her waist, but that simple touch seemed to travel all the way to her clit by the way it suddenly throbbed. Tristan could talk about one part of her body, and she could almost feel him touching her there...

"Stop! Just stop it!" she gasped, covering her burning cheeks. If he kept talking, she was going to... well she didn't know, but something was going to happen, and she'd end up embarrassing herself.

"Very well, I'll go easy on you. Just dinner tonight." He winked, and she could almost hear him say, *"Seduction tomorrow."*

There was something eerie and erotic about the way he studied her and drank again, licking his lips.

Every instinct inside Kat shouted that she was being hunted. It was the only word to describe the feeling. Every sense, every muscle was ramped up. Her heart beat hard against her ribs. She sucked in a breath as her body responded with interest. Too much interest. Her thighs quivered, and she pressed them together as she felt a flood of heat deep within her core. The idea that he wanted her was exciting, even thrilling. He made her feel...like a real woman. Yet she was still afraid to rush headlong into whatever this thing was between them. He seemed so confident and at ease about this, but she was spiraling out of her comfort zone at a hundred miles an hour. He probably did this whole "Here's dinner, let's have sex" routine with tons of girls all the time, but she didn't want to be just one of a string of women.

If it was casual sex, she'd regret it, and she didn't want any regrets. Sex was supposed to be meaningful, at least it was to her, and intimacy wasn't just physical —it should be emotional, too. Several of her friends from high school had told her about casual sex, but it hadn't seemed wonderful, not in the way Kat knew sex should be. It was part of the reason why she'd waited. For the right man at the right time. Was Tristan the one?

All her life she'd felt like a little girl, abandoned by her mother and at odds with the world around her. But when Tristan looked at her as he was doing now, she seemed to feel differently. Like the woman she wanted to be, one who knew herself and her own desires. As infuriating as it was to know he thought he would easily seduce her, she did want him to try because she wanted to kiss him again. To feel that heady rush of physical pleasure and that deeper sensation of connection.

When he kissed her, her mind seemed to flood with images of butterflies, of stained glass, of adventures from the books she cherished. He seemed to make everything she cared about come to life inside her mind. Like a wonderful sort of magic. It was easy to lose herself in the sensation of his embrace and leap off the edge without thinking. But what if he didn't feel the same way? The thought of being a notch on his bedpost made her feel a little anxious. But she'd pledged to herself she was busting out of her shell, and dinner with Tristan was certainly a risk she knew she should take.

"Fine. Dinner tonight," she said slowly, but she knew there might be more of something...maybe more kissing. She knew because her body and mind were warning her, warning her that she'd not last long against any sensual seduction. She might like whatever he did too much.

"Finish your dinner, and then we'll talk." Tristan towered over her until Kat was squirming.

Had he even realized he was bossing her around? It pissed her off, but it was also kind of a turn-on, and that *also* pissed her off. She didn't like men telling her what to do. But there was something about Tristan and the way he did it that made her annoyance melt and her body flush with heat. She could imagine other ways he could order her around. Like in bed...

"How are your classes?" he asked after she'd taken her first bite of the delicious pasta.

His desire to attempt to make small talk with her was almost funny. Was this his way of trying to date her? Did he think if he chatted her up, she'd be more open to whatever he clearly was thinking would come next? The heated looks Tristan was sending her way gave her the impression that he was picturing how she'd taste if he nibbled on her. She pictured him doing just that, and the dirty thoughts that followed made her heart skip.

How did he have this effect on her? It was as though whenever he came near her, he flipped some "sexy" switch inside her, and she wanted to kiss him... and do a whole lot more. With a swallow, she tried to breathe and not let her face heat up.

"You're really going to try and do the whole small talk thing with me after declaring you're going to seduce me?"

Tristan focused on his food as he took a bite, then looked up at her. "I like the sound of your voice. It's soft, husky. Like a woman well-loved in bed. If I can get you to keep talking, it doesn't matter what we talk about."

He liked the sound of her voice? Kat involuntarily reached up and touched her throat. When she realized what she'd done, she dropped her hand and gripped her plate of food. No matter what he said, small talk was safe. She could do that.

"Okay...we can talk. You asked about my classes. They've been good. I've had a lot of reading to do for exams."

"And what do you study? Have you selected a focus area?" He seemed genuinely interested, and she was actually glad to talk about it.

"History." She took a sip of her wine and then another bite of the food. It tasted as good as she'd imagined.

"Ahh, and what makes you like history? What do you plan to do with such an expertise?" The muscles of his forearms rippled when he picked up his plate again, and Kat had to collect herself before she could answer.

"I...uh, I want to teach. I plan to get a PhD. When I was little, I had a teacher who let us reenact the signing of the Magna Carta. Ever since then, I've been hooked. The stories about people from hundreds and thousands of years ago," she paused, realizing she was rambling, and ducked her head.

Tristan leaned forward and rested his elbows on his knees. "Please, don't stop. Finish what you were saying." There was an earnestness to his expression that compelled her to continue.

"Well, it's hard to explain but reading about people long after they're gone, it makes me feel less alone." She shouldn't have admitted that. It made her sound lonely, but it was the truth.

"That makes sense. I enjoy history for the same reasons."

Needing to change the subject, she turned the focus onto him.

"What about you? You said you were pursuing a Master's degree in business. I bet those classes are hard."

Tristan chuckled, leaning back in her desk chair. "It's been a challenge, but one I've enjoyed. Most people cringe when they think of finance and accounting or investment strategies. I enjoy all of that." Passion filled his face and, for a moment, it was hard to breathe.

He was so damn sexy, almost *too sexy*. A hint of a devastatingly perfect dimple peeped out from his left cheek when he smiled. She'd never had a thing for dimples, but his made her knees go weak. Resting a hand over her stomach, she tried to quell the rising flutter of excitement.

"What's the matter?"

"What'd you mean?" She licked her lips and glanced away.

"Your face is an enticing shade of pink." He poured himself a second glass of wine, but when she reached for her own empty glass, he shook a finger at her. "Oh no, one is enough for you. I want your wits about you when I'm around."

"What?" What man would ever refuse to let a girl drink more than one glass of wine? He was probably the first guy in the history of the world who didn't want a woman intoxicated to increase his chances of getting laid.

"I want every decision you make with me to be completely clear-headed."

"Why?" she demanded.

"Because I want you, Kat. And I want you to come to me without the influence of alcohol."

Kat swallowed hard. Come to him? "You mean *if* I sleep with you." She cleared her throat.

"*When* you sleep with me."

She gaped. Words dissolved on her tongue.

"Why do you look so surprised?" There was an edge to his voice that made her shiver, but not in a bad way.

Damn him.

"I'm trying to figure out how your head doesn't explode from the oversized ego you're carrying around."

"My massive ego? Trust me, it's not my ego that's oversized." He chuckled. "How many men have you been with?"

"That's none of your business," she shot back.

It was too personal. There was no way she was telling him she was virgin. No way in hell.

"A couple?" he guessed, and then his eyes narrowed. "One man?"

Still, she didn't answer. Her tongue seemed glued to the roof of her mouth.

"Are you a virgin?" He seemed to choke on the word.

Anger snapped inside her like a taut rubber band. "And if I am? Is that a bad thing?"

He needed to understand that she was cautious. Not some girl who slept with just any guy. Even if he was hot enough to melt her panties.

Shit! Get control, Kat.

"It's not a bad thing." Tristan stroked his jaw with one hand as he studied her. "It explains your reactions to me a bit more. Did you ever come close with someone?"

When she didn't answer, he spoke again. "Don't go quiet on me now, I like it when you aren't afraid. Talk to me," he pressed gently. "I promise not to tease you too much no matter what you say." He seemed genuine enough that she believed him, in this, at least.

She couldn't get the heat to fade from her face. "I had a boyfriend in high school, but we never did anything."

"Ahh, there it is." His lips sported a knowing smirk. Tristan relaxed, crossing his arms over his chest.

"What do you mean by that?" She climbed off her bed, stalked to the tiny counter, and clanged her plate as she set it down.

"Only that you don't have enough experience to recognize what there is between us."

He rose and joined her by the sink, setting his own plate on top of hers.

The heat of his body cocooned her when she turned around to face him. Right now, Kat hated how tall he was, how uneven she felt when trying to challenge him. The man could unbalance her with a smile, or a small but seductive brush of his hand anywhere on her body.

"There's nothing wrong with not having a lot of sexual experience. It means I'll have the pleasure of teaching you." His voice dropped to a husky level that sent ripples of excitement through her. "Of being your *first*. And there's so much I can introduce you to...toys...role play..." He made a soft, rumbling sound that was almost a growl.

"T—toys?" The word came out on a stutter, and she clamped her mouth shut.

"Yes. Things I can slip inside you that vibrate, pulse, shiver. Things that will make you lose your mind while I fuck you. Wouldn't you like that?"

It was like the power went out inside her head, and everything logical shut down as her body reacted with an explosion of lust. She rushed for the bed, sitting down just a second before her legs would have given out. Holy hell...She was talking to Tristan about sex toys?

He swirled his glass of wine, inhaling the scent, his lids dropping to half-mast.

Kat desperately needed another drink if they were going to continue this conversation. Lunging for his glass, she tore it from his grasp and downed the wine before he could stop her.

"That's enough," he reprimanded, prying the empty glass from her hands.

His full, oh-so-kissable lips were wilted in a frown as he set the glass on the small dresser. Then he placed his hands on her hips, his long elegant fingers spanning her waist.

The touch was intimate, but not overtly sexual,

but it didn't stop a stab of sharp arousal within her, and tingles of awareness flowing through her lower body.

"There is nothing wrong with limited experience." He moved one hand off her hip to raise her chin. "But you have no idea what it could be like between us. I knew from one kiss."

Kat didn't move away. The dark part of herself, the one she buried deep inside, unfurled like a red rose, petals curving out, ready to be touched, caressed by the words Tristan spoke.

"What did you know?" She stared at his lips, remembering all too well that kiss. The one in the bar, but the others, too. Every kiss with him was stunning, but she'd thought that was just her. If *he* felt that way too...

"When I kiss you, it makes me forget my name." He stroked a fingertip over her lips, tracing their shape. "I can't seem to get you out of my head. I've had dozens of women and yet you..." He paused as though puzzled. "You're all I can think about. Don't deny you feel something too. Aren't you curious?"

8

"**A**ren't you curious?"

The question left Tristan's lips in a seductive almost-whisper, and that dark part of herself purred, begging to be released.

"But we don't even know each other. I can't sleep with someone I don't know." Was she really even considering sleeping with him? They shouldn't be having this discussion. Whatever happened to old-fashioned dating? Kat almost laughed. She couldn't picture Tristan dating or doing anything so *normal*. He didn't look normal, didn't act normal, was the farthest *thing* from normal.

Tristan cupped her cheek and leaned down to whisper in her ear. "If that's all it takes, then let's get to know each other." He dropped his hands to his waist, lifting his sweater to unhook his belt and slide it out from the loops.

"What are you doing?"

"You can use it to restrain me, bind one of my hands to the bed railing." He pointed to the slender metal frame jutting out an inch past her mattress. "It will keep you safe from me seducing you. At least tonight. Normally I'm the one who likes to restrain a woman in bed, but in situations for building trust..."

He stroked the soft-looking black leather of the belt. "I'll let you bind me to the bed. Just one hand. I can't do anything to you except lay beside you. We can talk, get to know each other."

"That sounds like bundling from colonial America." She remembered reading about it in high school, where couples courting would be allowed to spend the night. The man would be sewn up in a sackcloth so the couple couldn't be intimate physically.

He laughed. "It's a mite better than sewing me up in a sackcloth, but yes, the principle is much the same. I knew you Americans had some good ideas."

A laugh escaped her, and she couldn't stop it. "Are you always this ridiculous?"

Tristan winked at her. "If it makes you laugh, then I'll be ridiculous more often." His gaze softened then. "I like it when you laugh, it's a nice sound."

The sincere compliment caught her off guard, and that familiar heat that always followed Tristan's praise flooded through her body.

"Thanks. I like the way you laugh too." *God, now I sound ridiculous.* But it was true, his laughter was wonderful to her ears. It was rich, almost melodic, and it instantly made her want to smile. There was never anything forced about his humor, nor was it mean. Some guys she'd known in the past only found things funny when people got hurt or when it was at someone else's expense. Tristan may have had an innate sense of self-importance, but he didn't have any cruelty or coldness to him. Rather he drew her in with his smiles, his teasing, and his laughter. It made him irresistible.

"Well, what do you say? I'm up for a bit of bundling." He flashed that wicked grin that made her knees go weak.

Giggling, she shook her head. "I was sort of in the middle of studying. I don't have time to play kinky sex games with you." It scared her how appealing that idea really was, though. Sure the man had sex appeal just rolling off him in waves, but she also had to admit she really liked talking to him, just being around him. It was fun and engaging. It felt like the beginning of a bigger adventure than anything on her list would ever be. If she kept spending time with him, she'd want something more, like a real relationship, but she knew from what she and Lacy had discovered about his past that he wasn't a relationship kind of guy. He went from woman to woman, bed to bed. That wasn't a guy you could depend on to be a steady boyfriend. That was a guy who would break your heart. No smart woman would sign up for that willingly. Still... Tristan was so irresistible that she couldn't seem to convince herself to stop this thing between them from going any further.

"Kinky sex games are actually my specialty. Just wait until I get you tied down on a bed...the things I can do when you're spread helpless and I have all night to play with you..." He let that image float through the silence that followed, and Kat struggled for breath.

*Tied down...Tristan's body over hers...helpless to stop whatever he might do...*Kat's body quaked with a sudden, almost painful surge of lust.

And then he was standing right in front of her, one hand touching her waist again, and the other cupping her chin. "You'd better remember to breathe, you're turning red, darling."

Breathe? How can I breathe when I'm thinking about you dominating me in bed?

She forced air into her lungs, shocked to find out she really hadn't been breathing for the last several seconds. Tristan traced a fingertip over her lips, his intense gaze following its path as though he was fascinated. Most men stared at a girl's breasts, or her ass, but not him. When Tristan stared at her mouth, she felt like he was thinking of a thousand erotic things he could do to her lips, and the possibilities sent bolts of electric awareness through her, turning her into a sexual livewire.

"Can we not talk about sex?" she begged him and gently pushed his hand away from her mouth. She instantly missed his touch, but she knew she had to keep her head on straight to say what she needed to say.

"Why not?" His eyes narrowed slightly. "It happens to be one of my favorite things."

She snorted. "I can tell, but it's really distracting me, okay? And I need to be focused on school and classes and not..." She waved a hand between their bodies.

"I thought you liked me?" He seemed puzzled.

Kat blew out a frustrated breath. "That's the problem! I like you too much. You're bad for me, Tristan."

With a responding laugh, he checked his watch, eyed her stack of books, and then winked at her. "Perhaps I am bad for you, but everybody needs a weakness now and then, a guilty pleasure. Otherwise life isn't worth living. Now, why don't you take the rest of the night off? *Live* a little."

How did he know just what buttons to push? "Sleeping with you is living? Is that what you're saying?" *Why do I have to sound so breathless as I say this?* Kat wanted to smack herself, but damn if her heart didn't trip over a few beats at the thought of being in bed with him.

"I'm saying that what we could have is worth exploring, and one night of putting the books aside won't do you any harm."

Her focus fixed on the belt, noticing the silver buckle again. Was he seriously into kinky stuff? Kat hadn't ever given thought to wild, edgy sex, but now that she was faced with Tristan and his belt, a flutter of excitement stirred in her belly.

"I suggest that you let me stay the night, and we get to know each other. Whatever happens, happens. But *you* will be in full control."

She bit her lip.

Can I do this? Bind this man to my bed? Her blood heated at the thought. If he couldn't do anything, couldn't overwhelm her, she would feel safe. His boldness, his natural domination excited her, but she was afraid of how much he affected her. Opening herself up to someone who could make her feel such strong emotions and have such strong physical reactions to was dangerous to her body...and her heart.

"One night, Kat. Give me one night to prove it's worth whatever risks you think you must take. If you still have reservations in the morning, I'll let you go your way and I'll go mine." The man's smooth words and the curve of his sensual lips were tempting.

She felt like Eve staring at her reflection in the glossy, ruby red surface of an apple in the garden. Temptation. *Pure, wicked, temptation.* That was Tristan to his core.

Kat had never been tempted before, not like this. Nothing had ever broken through that carefully guarded fortress she'd built when her mother left. Yet this man, like mist, seemed to seep through the walls of stone and fill every part of her mind with thoughts, and her body with surging desires.

Kat nibbled her lip, sensing that neither of them could walk away now, not until they'd tried this.

She was afraid to ask how far it would go. One night in bed? One night of making love, or did he intend to go beyond that? Was he serious about seeing her again after this? Like actually dating? Her head told her no, that he wasn't wanting anything more than to satisfy his own curiosity, but that little voice inside her heart whispered something entirely different.

What if he really does like me and wants to see if something between us could work? Sure he's a rich, titled aristocrat, and I'm not, but what if we found a way to make none of that matter?

She wished she knew what his true intentions were. Until she did, everything inside her would be off balance, teetering on the edge of a cliff and praying she wouldn't fall.

"If we do this—" she held up a hand to keep him from speaking "—and I say I'm not interested in you tomorrow morning, what happens then?"

He lowered the belt, a solemn expression darkening his eyes like summer storm clouds. "Then I walk away, but you have to honestly mean it."

That should have relieved her, but a heavy weight settled on her shoulders, and a knot of anxiety grew in her chest, digging into her heart like a wild briar's thorns. The truth was she didn't want him to walk away. Ever since she'd had the courage to go up and stand next to him at the bar, and they'd talked, she'd felt comfortable around him and fascinated by him. He wasn't just a gorgeous man with a sense of humor, he was also smart and deep. She could count on one hand the number of men she'd met with whom she could check all those boxes. A girl couldn't just let a man like him walk away, not when everything about him felt so...*right*.

Taking a deep breath, she gave him a shaky nod. "Okay, let's give this a try."

Please don't let this be a mistake.

Tristan's lips curved. "Excellent." He glanced at his watch. It looked expensive, with its black leather band and black onyx face with gold Roman numerals. Understated, elegant, and sexy. Like him.

Lacy had been right. He was the sort of man a woman actually melted from when they got too close to him. Like a beam of summer sunlight, he cut straight through Kat, heating her up from the inside with just a look or a twitch of those kissable lips.

"It's getting late. I assume you have an early class tomorrow?"

She nodded. "History of the Russian Monarchy from 1400 to the Red Revolution."

A little smile curled his lips. "Well, that would certainly wake me up in the morning," he teased. "Why don't you change into your pajamas. I'll use the lavatory, and then we can get into bed."

Kat stared at him, then at her bed. "This is so crazy," she muttered before opening her dresser and grabbing a warm pair of cotton plaid pajama pants and a loose T-shirt. Not sexy, but she didn't own anything sexy. Now she wished she had something sheer and silky...something that would make him kiss her again. She wanted to have what Lacy and Mark had, that pull to someone else that made it impossible to stay away from them. Drawn together by gravity.

"You really want to stay here?" she asked Tristan, clutching her pajamas and feeling silly that she hoped he would say yes.

Tristan took his time in answering as he walked up to her. She had to tilt her head back a little to look up into his penetrating blue-green eyes.

"A woman who tells something true about herself in the middle of a pub, who is brave enough to confess such a secret to a stranger, that's a woman worth knowing. I want to be here, I want to know you, Kat. What makes you tick, what you think about, what your hopes and dreams are...you are fascinating to me." He bit his bottom lip, as though almost puzzled at his own curiosity.

"Talking about butterflies and books doesn't make

me brave," she argued, but her tone was soft. They were almost whispering, standing so close. She couldn't seem to stay away from him, but did he feel that same way about her?

Tristan brushed his fingers through her hair, tucking one stray lock behind her left ear. "Do you know that I've never had a truly meaningful conversation with any woman aside from my cousin Celia or my mother? Not until you. What you've told me...it is brave to open yourself to someone else, and I don't mean physically, although that's certainly brave, too." He chuckled.

"You really think I'm brave?" She wanted so badly to hear him say yes.

"I do. You're incredible, Kat. You're real in a way so many other women aren't. I want to know you better. So yes, I'm staying the night." He leaned his head down, and she waited eagerly for a kiss, but he nuzzled her cheek, and his hands settled on her shoulders, squeezing slightly.

When Kat rocked up on her toes, trying to kiss him, he pulled his face away, a dark cloud flashing across his eyes.

"If you kiss me, I'll lose control, darling. I've promised to be on my best behavior, but if you do that again, all bets are off."

The thought of him losing control always sent her heartbeat leaping. She was so nervous about having sex for the first time, but part of her trusted that Tristan might be the man to show her how wonderful it could be, if she was ready. Not tonight, but soon...

"I guess I should change..." She glanced down at her clothes then up at him.

"Of course." His voice was low, slightly husky as he backed away from her and headed for the bathroom.

She waited for him to shut the door, but when he

gazed at her a moment too long, she waved a hand at him.

"Go," she said, rolling her eyes, "I'm not changing in front of you."

With a wry chuckle, he shook his head. "I thought it might be worth a try." Tristan winked and disappeared into her small restroom.

Kat scrambled out of her clothes and into the pj's, not knowing how much time she had to change. But he took his time, and after she was dressed, she used the opportunity to study the gift he'd left on her desk. She picked up the box, weighing it in her hands. Was it *The Mysterious Island*? The box was the right size, and the weight seemed like it was possible. Kat gave it a little shake but whatever was inside didn't shift or make any sound.

Drat! She set it back down on the desk and folded her arms over her chest.

When he came back out, still in his jeans and sweater, he smirked at the sight of her sitting on the edge of the bed.

"Did you peek?" He nodded toward the blue wrapped package.

"No." She raised her chin, pretending to be offended. It had been tempting. *Really tempting.*

"You wanted to, though, didn't you?" he teased.

She laughed and shrugged. "I did, and you *knew* I would want to." She couldn't help but smile.

"Go on, open it." He waited for her to move.

Kat rose from the bed and approached the box. Her hands hesitated inches from the black bow.

"If I open this, there are no strings attached, right?" She didn't want to be a woman who took gifts from a man in exchange for...well...sex. Even if she might desperately want to have sex with him, she didn't want it to be out of obligation.

"No strings. I wanted to get this for you, from one

collector to another." He seemed sincere, but it was impossible not to notice when Tristan picked up the ribbon and wrapped it around one fist, tugging it tight against his skin as though he were testing it as a way to bind something or someone...like her. But he didn't. He played with the ribbon, spooling it around his fingers, the silk whispering against his skin.

When he cleared his throat, she came back to herself with a little shake and unwrapped the box. As she lifted the lid, she gasped and stepped back.

Dropped from the Clouds was nestled in the tissue paper, the gilded balloon on the cover gleaming in the dim light from the desk lamp.

"Oh my God," Kat whispered, then her eyes flew to his. "This is the one from G. David's bookshop, isn't it?" She'd known he'd bought it, but she still hadn't been prepared for him to actually give it to her.

"How did you know?" One dark brow arched up.

With a quick swallow, she reached into the box for the book, almost afraid to touch it.

"My friend heard they'd received an order for the book. I couldn't resist looking, so I went to the shop this morning. I asked the clerk if you bought it. She sort of hinted that you did, without actually saying it." Her head spun when she remembered the price tag. "Tristan, this cost more than fifteen hundred dollars. I can't accept anything that expensive." She reached for the box lid, but he dropped the ribbon and caught her wrist.

"Don't think of the money. Consider it a gift from one enthusiast to another."

"You collect antique books?" she asked, stunned. He didn't seem the type, but at this point, she really didn't know him at all, did she?

"Not books, maps. I like old ones. G. David's has an excellent cartography selection in their rare book room. I enjoy books, of course, but maps are my obsession." His eyes were so warm, like the waters in Bermuda.

Her father had taken her there for a few months when she was twelve. The hot beaches, the warm water, a sense of endless heaven. In that moment, Tristan's gaze, so hot and tender, filled her with that rare sense of wonder. How could one man's gaze have the same effect as an island paradise?

"Why do you like maps?" she asked softly.

He picked up the leather belt and walked over to the bed. The little twirl in the air he made with his belt was flirtatious, sexy, and yet almost funny.

"Tie me up, darling, and I'll spill all my secrets."

9

"All of your secrets?" Kat approached Tristan grinning. "Dare I ask what *sort* of secrets you have to spill?"

"Only the best kind of secrets." He sat down on the edge of her bed and she couldn't resist coming a few steps closer.

"That's not an answer. What kind of secrets? Don't hold out on me, Kingsley," she challenged, using his last name in the way she'd seen the local boys at Cambridge tease each other.

"Oh, Kingsley, is it? Call me Tristan, and I'll tell you *anything* you want."

"Anything?" She put her finger to her chin and pretended to contemplate that.

"Anything," he promised, his eyes blazing with that intensity that sent showers of invisible sparks rippling beneath her skin.

"How about a request instead?" she asked.

"Very well, name it." Again, he had that kingly air about him, but it didn't frustrate her as it had earlier. She was coming to understand him, this enigma of a man. Beneath the expensive clothes and that gorgeous body, there was a man who had been raised to be a leader among men. It awed her, and a flutter of excitement and nervousness filled her stomach.

"Could I see your signet ring?"

His brows raised, but he wordlessly removed his ring from his left little finger and dropped it into her outstretched palm. Kat studied the ring. Two unicorns arched over a shield containing three doves and a harp. It was such a small engraving on the ring, but she could still make it out.

"What's it like...being titled? I mean—" she fumbled for the right words "—knowing that someday you'll be the Earl of Pembroke?" She placed the ring back on his open palm.

A contemplative silence kept him quiet for a moment as he slid the ring back on his finger, his head bowed as he sighed. When he looked at her again, she saw an ancient seriousness in his eyes that filled her with sadness. It was a look of someone trapped by knowing that their life held a certain amount of obstacles before them, ones they couldn't avoid. An acceptance of an inevitability.

"It weighs heavy upon the heart," he replied and tapped his chest with a closed fist. It reminded her of the old movies she'd watched with her father where knights saluted their kings before rushing into battle on their gallant white chargers.

"I'm sorry." She hated that he felt that way, she couldn't begin to imagine the duties, the expectations, the demands of that life. It was so far removed from her own.

Tristan rolled his shoulders in a loose gesture. "It isn't your fault." A smile kissed the corners of his lips. "You Americans are so delightful, always apologizing for things out of your control." He reached up and curled his fingers around her hand, squeezing it before he let go.

"Now, quit distracting me, I'm trying to get into your bed, you little minx."

"Minx?" Now she couldn't stop the giggles. Only someone like him would call a woman a minx. And she loved it.

He bent over to untie the laces of his boots and removed them. Then he placed his wrist against the metal railing and curled a finger from his other hand at her to come closer. The simple action flushed her entire body with heat. What would it be like to have him beckoning her to bed when they were both naked and—

"You'll have to wrap securely it, since I can't do it one-handed." He waited for her to cross the last few feet of space that separated them.

Kat leaned down and circled the belt around the metal railing halfway down the bed. It wouldn't be too uncomfortable for him to lie on the bed with his hand tied by his upper thigh.

"Okay, done." She stepped back.

Tristan gave a few quick hard jerks on the leather and then looked up at her. He had some mobility in his body, but because of his wrist he couldn't get away from the bed. They were only a few feet apart, and he was partially restrained, yet she still felt like he was the one in control. It disturbed and excited her.

"I'm at your mercy, Kat, darling, whatever will you do with me?"

His soft British accent had devastating consequences to her libido. She clenched her thighs together and sucked in a breath, trying to focus and not just jump his bones like her body was screaming to do.

"'Do with you'? Where to start?" She tapped her chin with a finger, a gleeful smile on her lips. Shocked by her playfulness, his lips parted and his eyes darkened.

"Remember, darling, I've only got so much control," he warned, a wolfish expression making him that much more dangerous...to her innocence.

"Hmmm, in that case, I want you to promise me you won't snore, I can't stand that," she said with a giggle.

"That I can promise. No snoring," he vowed with a humorous false solemnity.

"Good. Do you need anything, like a glass of water? An extra pillow?" Kat eyed the narrow bed, trying to picture how they would share it.

I guess we'll get friendly real fast. She bit the inside of her cheek to keep from laughing at the absurdity of the situation.

"All I need is for you to lie down beside me so we can talk." He patted the bed with his free hand.

Kat swallowed and forced herself to move. She turned off all of the lights except for the lamp on her nightstand before she turned back to face him.

Tristan had stolen one of her two pillows and was lying back, his free hand propped behind his head in a relaxed pose. He had just enough mobility to achieve that. And he looked...sinfully tempting. His long, lean, muscled body, stretched out on her bed beneath the covers, reminded her of a jaguar lounging on the branch of a tree.

"Are we really doing this?" Hope colored her tone, and she prayed she didn't sound silly by how excited she was at sharing a bed with him.

"I want you, Kat. If you and I need to get to know each other first for you to trust me, then I'm game for that. The question is, are you brave enough to get to know me?"

His voice echoed in her head. *I'll tell you all my secrets.* What sort of secrets could someone like Tristan have?

She walked over to the empty side of the little

bed and pulled back the covers, sliding underneath them. She'd never been this close to any man, not even Ben. The idea of Tristan sleeping beside her the whole night made her nervous, but she felt safe, too. And that had nothing to do with him being half tied up.

Tristan remained on his back, free arm behind his head. "Ask me anything, Kat." He stared up at the ceiling, as though awaiting some grand interrogation.

She snuggled deeper into her bed, and into him. The bed was tiny and just big enough for the two of them if they touched shoulder to feet. She tried to resist the urge to get too close, but it was impossible. Kat finally surrendered to his warmth and leaned into his body while she ran through a list of questions in her head.

"Why do you like old maps?"

He chuckled, then blew out a slow breath before speaking. "Maps are like pictures. They capture a moment in time, a specific point in history. But it's more than that. They unlock the past and show the way people and nations viewed the world. How borders were drawn, what countries were named...it's a guide to the way people used to think, on a massive scale." A wry smile twisted his lips.

Kat found nothing silly about it. He was absolutely right, and that depth and insight by him fascinated her.

"My turn," he said. "Why do you like books?"

She laughed. "That's your question? Out of all of the things you could ask? I've already told you that."

"I mean, aside from what you told me last night, there's more to it, isn't there?" And just like that, Kat realized he truly did understand her, deep inside. How could a man she barely knew seem to know her so well?

She studied his profile, the aquiline nose, sensual

lips, strong jaw. He had all of the things that made a man sexy and yet it wasn't just his looks.

It was the way he acted, especially toward her. His voice, pitched soft and low, made her hungry for dark, wicked, sinful things. His body, the heat of it, made her want to curl up against him. And his eyes, those stunning eyes, cut right through her. As though he could see straight into her, every dream and desire. And then there was the way he talked, the things he said, as though in some distant time their two souls had been connected. Like soul mates rediscovering each other.

How can I feel this way toward him? I barely know him? But it was the truth, she felt like she'd known him for years.

Tristan turned to her, those eyes boring into her. "Books are a part of you, Katherine. It is the most important thing I could ask you, to bare part of your soul." He brushed his knuckles over her cheek. She closed her eyes, relishing the way her skin tingled wherever he touched her.

"So tell me, what do you *really* love about books?" he repeated, gently but firmly.

Kat propped her head up on her pillow and slowly reached out and placed her hand on his chest. The fabric of his thin sweater was soft, and his heat warmed her palm. His heartbeat was slow, steady, reassuring. Her own was fast and wild in comparison. Had he done this with other girls? Was this normal for him? The very idea that she wasn't the first for him cut her deep. She wanted to be doing something with him that he hadn't done with anyone else. She wanted whatever they did together to be special.

"I'll answer your question if you answer something else for me."

"Very well, I'll indulge you." He smiled.

"How many times have you done this with other girls?"

His smile faded. "By *this* you mean what?"

"This." She waved a hand at their bodies.

He covered her hand that lay on his chest and stroked her fingers. "Kat, I've been with other women, but I've never let one tie to me to a bed, nor have I simply stayed the night to talk to them."

"Really?" She swallowed hard.

"Yes, darling. I'm willing to do anything to be with you."

"In bed." Her tone came out with a little more bite than she intended. When he didn't correct her, she added, "I can't figure out if that's an insult or a compliment." She pulled her hand away from his body, but he grabbed her wrist and put her palm back on his chest. He stroked the back of her hand with his fingertips. The touch was lulling, almost hypnotic.

"It's a compliment. I'm beginning to realize that with you, none of my normal rules apply."

He continued to brush his fingers over her skin, and that touch seemed more intimate than any kiss they'd shared.

"Now tell me why you love books. I've been honest with you. Please be honest with me." His compelling gaze forced Kat to admit she owed him that.

"Books..." She thought through her response, and his fingers curled tighter around hers in a gentle squeeze. That touch gave her the strength to confess. "Books are safe. You don't have to say good-bye. They don't hurt you, or leave you." She didn't raise her gaze until she was done. When their eyes met, her breath caught in her throat.

A flash of deep emotions moved behind his eyes, a lightning storm behind rain-darkened clouds.

"I want to kiss you right now." His low tone

scraped her senses like the old wood of an antique desk her father had once owned. Enticing, and a little rough. She licked her lips, wanting to give in but not wanting to make the first move.

"Then do it," she challenged, her own voice husky. Every muscle in her body was tense, her body aching for the promise of Tristan's slowly spreading grin. How could his smile make such a promise? Like *I'm going to own you, possess every part of you, and you'll never want to be free.*

He used his free hand to slide underneath her body, urging her to lean over him a little.

She rolled up over him, the covers still around them, then held still, holding her breath as she waited. The slow sweet anticipation of his mouth rising to hers sent delicious quivers through her.

A faint brush of lips, an exhalation of shared breaths, and then he was kissing her. Slowly, deliberately, as though he wanted to memorize every part of her lips. It began as a low burn, like a fire in the heart of winter, heating up with each pop and crack of wood, each flick of his tongue against the seam of her lips, entreating her to open with sweet surrender.

Butterflies swirled in her stomach and she shivered, trying to quell her nerves, but she couldn't deny the excitement at being kissed, *tasted* by this gorgeous man. She could drown in the delightful sensations his touch created.

His kiss was dark and rich, like chocolate and soft black velvet with a hint of wine, wood-smoked and subtle, but oh so deep. There was nothing beyond his mouth and the contact of their bodies.

She needed more, craved it like a wild beast driven only by instinct. Her hands slid up his chest, clawing his sweater, feeling the bulge and slide of his muscles as he responded to her touch. Kat gripped his shoulder and neck, her hands latching onto him, desperate to drag him closer, pull herself over him more.

A distant creak, a little tug, a growl of frustration, and she slowed in her sensual assault. He was bound, couldn't move, couldn't touch her the way she wanted him to.

Creak.

The subtle sound of his struggle, as though he wasn't even aware of it, heated her blood that much more. He was obeying his own code, not demanding that she set him free. He had promised to stay bound, so she felt safe.

I am safe. Every instinct shouted that. *Can I let him go?*

His lips drifted to her jaw, caressing her neck, until she was lost in the heat of his body and his kiss again.

"Tristan," she murmured against his neck, trying to catch his attention.

"Hmm?" A soft vibration of his response against her throat made her shiver again.

"I can let you free if—"

"No," he whispered. "If you free me, I won't be able to control myself. I'm dying to pin you beneath me and fuck you to within an inch of your life." He arched up a little to nip her neck.

*Oh, God...*She wanted it, to hell with her reservations about not sleeping with him so soon. She needed to get closer to him, to feel their bodies skin-to-skin, mouths and hands exploring each other. *I want him to lose control.*

The mental image he painted sent pleasurable shock waves through her. Kat took control, shoving him down hard so he fell flat on his back.

Have to kiss him.

Driven by pure basic hunger, she didn't let her cautious nature win this time. She pushed back the covers and climbed on top of him. She was undoing the belt from his wrist before she let herself think it through. She kissed his parted lips, reveling in the fact that she had temporarily shocked him. But it didn't last long. The belt dropped to the ground with a soft thump.

Tristan curled his now-free arm around her waist and rolled their bodies, pinning her beneath him on his side of the bed. He gripped her wrists and yanked them above her head, trapping them in one of his hands

"Should've warned you, darling," he murmured. "I can't resist a challenge." Then Tristan kissed her again, holding her helpless beneath him, but Kat wasn't afraid.

Anxious, excited, aroused, but not afraid.

"Tell me to stop," he ordered in between kisses. "Tell me to stop, and I will. I promised tonight would be just talking...not this."

But she didn't want him to stop.

"No, I want this...I want you." Letting him take control made her feel so hot, a sheen of sweat coated her body. Being flush under Tristan as he overwhelmed her senses was beyond hot.

He seduced her with his mouth, through an erotic play of lips and tongue, torturing her with a promise of what was to come.

Her thighs quivered, and wet heat pooled between them. Panting, aching, she was wriggling against him in silent encouragement. Tristan's hand slid down her side, teasing her sensitive waist before he flattened his palm on her stomach and slipped it under the loose band of her pajama bottoms and into her underwear. When he cupped her mound possessively, his fingers probing at her folds, she hissed against his lips.

Kat arched her back, pushing his fingers deeper into her.

She hadn't known it could feel...*powerful*.

Being with Tristan was wild, out of control, searing hot. He seemed to know what to do, just what to say to make her lose her mind.

She didn't want him to stop. Ever.

✹ 10 ✺

"**F**uck!" Tristan struggled to remain in control. He had Kat pinned beneath him, her wrists trapped under his hand as his other hand penetrated that sweet, tight little sheath, and he was about to lose his mind. All he wanted to do was be on top of her, skin-to-skin, as close as he could get. Having her under his control, letting him have the power to show her how good he could make her feel... it made *him* feel too damn good. If only he could be inside her, really fucking her, not just with his hand... he would be in nirvana. As it was, he was barely clinging to the shreds of his sanity.

One finger...that was all he could get inside her. Liquid heat burned his skin as his finger fucked her, slow and steady. He'd have to work on stretching her before he got inside her. She was too small, too unused to the type of wild and often rough sex he craved, but he could give her a release tonight, show her a taste of what he wanted, what *she* wanted, too.

"Oh, God, that feels—" Kat whimpered in pleasure as he curled his index finger inside her, finding that hidden spot that every woman had.

It was a tiny little place, feeling almost rough to his touch. Using the pad of his index finger, he curled it repeatedly over that spot. Kat's legs spasmed around his hips, and she nearly crushed his arm between their bodies as she thrashed when the orgasm hit her hard. She moaned, the heavy, throaty purr tensing every muscle in his body.

Fuck. He needed to come. Needed to get inside her before his arousal killed him.

When she threw her head back, her long, dark brown hair felt like silk on his hand.

It was the last thing he needed. He came right then and there in his trousers, like a bloody schoolboy. The embarrassment over his lack of control would hit him later, but right then he didn't care. Pleasure exploded through him, like volts of electricity, shocking everything inside him until he broke apart.

The intense pleasure faded, and an unfamiliar urge rapidly took its place. He stared at Kat, their noses brushing, his body jerking and trembling as he slowly drifted down from that glorious high. All he wanted was to stay right there in her bed, looking at her, holding her, feeling her close.

Never in his life had that ever been in his mind right after sex. *Ever*.

He cleared his throat. "Would you mind if I got up for a minute? I need to take care of a little matter." For the first time since he was a lad, his cheeks burned as he rolled off her and waited for her to nod. He rubbed his wrist as he stood up, a red stripe circling it from where the belt had dug in when he'd tugged on it.

"Do you have a large pair of boxers? Or shorts?"

"Yes." Kat stood and headed for the top drawer of her dresser, pulling out a pair of boxers.

They'd be snug, but they'd work for one night. He took them and hastily shut himself in her lavatory, stripping out of his clothes. He used a washcloth to clean himself and then slipped the boxers on. He placed his hands on opposites of the sink and stared into the little gilt-edged mirror.

His hair was mussed, his muscles tense, and he didn't recognize the odd expression on his face, as though he were half lost in a dream. A dream of pleasure and anticipation, and there was a hint of tenderness when he thought of Kat. His sweet little Kat.

Tristan understood her demand that they go beyond sex, at least enough for them to learn about one another. It made everything so much more...*intense* in bed. Knowing why she loved books, how he'd shared his obsession for maps, they'd opened up to each other. How much more intense could the sex be if they kept...sharing those secret parts of themselves?

He scraped a hand over his jaw, then gave his reflection a nod.

Give it a try.

Maybe learning more about a woman than her favorite style of lingerie and preferred sexual position was worth it.

This time. With this girl.

He exited the bathroom and froze when he saw Kat sitting on the edge of her bed, legs tucked up, chin resting on her knees as she watched him with wide eyes. Her long, luscious hair was a mess of wild waves about her shoulders. She looked like a tempting Siren, ready to lure him to his doom. All she was lacking were a pair of opalescent shells to cup her breasts and a shimmery tail with water beading on the delicate scales.

And just like that...he was hard again. What was it about this woman that made him lose himself so easily? The arousal was slow to fade, especially when he walked to the bed and cupped her cheeks in his hands. Those dark lashes of hers fanned up, followed by those lovely gray eyes. He'd never given much thought to the color, but hers was almost electric, like liquid mercury, sucking him in.

"Move over, darling. I'll take this side of the bed."

When she finally moved, he saw the lines of tension bracketing her mouth soften. So she thought he would just leave after what had happened? Not bloody likely. After she'd scooted over beneath the covers, he climbed in and clicked off the lamp on the nightstand. Without a second thought, he pulled her into his arms. She fit perfectly tucked against his body.

"I want to know everything about you," he murmured into her ear. "Your favorite color, your favorite ice cream, what makes your heart beat fast. *Everything.*" He kissed the soft shell of her ear.

She shivered. "Will you share the same with me?"

He chuckled. "Let's see. Navy blue, rocky road, you."

He waited for her to figure out what he'd just said.

"Wait, *I* make your heart beat fast?" Kat rolled onto her side to stare at him in the darkness. He could just barely make out her features. He took one of her hands and laid her palm flat on his chest above his heart.

"Feel that?" As he spoke his heartbeat sped up. "That's for you."

She nodded, looking away. She was still shy, after everything they'd done together? He rarely seduced women who were bashful, but something about Kat fascinated him. She raised her head. The moonlight, although faint, pooled in her eyes liked polished silver coins.

Kat shifted against him, her hand still on his chest. Her fingertips drew small circles on his skin, and he repressed a delicious shiver. He loved that she was brave enough to keep touching him.

I'm winning her over. A grin twisted his lips before he could stop himself, but she didn't seem to notice.

"Tristan, when we were at the Pickerel Inn you said stained glass made you cry. Why is that?"

Tristan debated a long moment on how to describe it. "The colors are so rich, they seem to burn right through the glass. And the faces of the people—their expressions are so clear, so sharp. Sometimes I feel like I can read the people in the glass better than I can read the people around me." Could he explain the other part, about how it'd helped him be strong as a lad? He'd never revealed that to anyone, but could he do that with her? He had a feeling he could...just the way she'd talked about the butterflies with him. Some things were too personal, but with her, he wanted to share.

"I know what you mean. People today seem to be so blank-faced. I like reading a person's eyes, seeing their facial expressions." Her lips curved up in a half-smile that he could just make out from his angle as he looked down at her nestled against him. Ever since he'd come to her room tonight, she'd been more and more comfortable around him, able to touch him back the way he touched her. Intimately, not just sexually. Not every caress from a lover should be given out of the desire for sex, even he knew that, although he'd never tried it himself. But with Kat it felt natural to hold her tightly while she stroked his chest. It felt...normal, in a strange sort of way that made him want to grin until his face hurt.

"Do you know what I see when I look at you?" He curled one finger under her chin and tipped her head back so he could see her face more clearly. She was so lovely it made something deep in him ache.

Kat licked her lips. "What do you see?"

"Besides a beautiful, sexy woman? I see someone

with secrets. Someone who wants to live but doesn't know how."

Her lashes lowered but she didn't shy away from him.

"There's nothing wrong with that, Kat. You're just getting out into the world to start living." He didn't want to hurt her, but he wanted only the truth between them. "Now it's your turn."

"Hmm..." She continued to trace teasing patterns on his skin. It amazed him that such an innocent touch could make his cock harder than any other woman's sensual touch.

"My favorite color is red. A sort of dark cranberry, almost burgundy. It's rich, warm..."

"Seductive?" He lifted her hand to his lips and pressed a kiss to the inside of her palm.

A swell of triumph filled him when her breath caught and she shivered. Tristan couldn't resist flicking his tongue out to lick her palm and he kissed it again.

"I think you just like saying that word to tease me," she giggled.

"Of course I do, teasing you is my new favorite hobby. I've never been one for hobbies, but this one I intend to cultivate." He feathered his lips on her hand again, smirking roguishly.

Another quick inhalation, and her eyelashes fluttered as she sighed.

It cost him everything to contain his own groan of painful pleasure. He wanted to be bullocks deep inside her, banging her into the bed so hard she couldn't breathe, but she wasn't ready. He could only pray that the wait wouldn't kill him.

"And ice cream?" he prompted, giving her a little distraction from his seduction.

"Chocolate. Simple, I know, but why mess with something when it's perfect the way it is?"

He laughed softly. "I agree. Not everything in life should be complicated. And the rest?"

She ducked her head again. "You make my heart beat fast."

"Aside from me. Though I rather enjoy knowing, of course." He moved one hand to her shoulder, then trailed a lazy fingertip across her collarbone. The skin beneath his fingers was satiny soft and a creamy, natural white he found enchanting after dating women who spent too much time in attaining fake tans.

"Listening to Russian composers, particularly Tchaikovsky and Rachmaninoff."

Rachmaninoff? The specificity of her interest, the unique taste, was so refreshing.

"What do you like about Russian music?"

She nibbled her lip. "Many European composers' music is mathematically precise, with repetitive patterns, where the sound is almost too perfect. Russian composers, at least during the nineteenth century, were different. They used music not only to tell a story, but to show a depth of emotion." She was touching his chest again, sliding her hand up and down as she talked. "The swells, the passion, the bittersweet despair, the hope, the love. It reverberates with every note—it sweeps you away."

Tristan held his breath, remembering how, the night before, he'd asked her if she wanted to be swept off her feet, and how she'd said she did. He lowered his head with the need to kiss her, not because he craved sex, but because he simply wanted to be close to her. To connect with her in a small way. Her mouth parted beneath his, and yet he didn't let the kiss turn rough. He deepened it gently, coaxing her to make love with her mouth.

Minutes later, he somehow found his way out of the sweet fog of desire.

She exhaled softly, then yawned.

"Are you tired?" Her answer was going to be obvious, but he delighted in making her admit it.

"A little." Her voice was barely above a murmur.

"Liar," he teased. "I can tell you're about to drift off. Why don't you get some sleep? I promise to only hold you tonight. Do you trust me?"

At his question she nodded like a sleepy kitten and snuggled deeper into his embrace. Tristan pulled the comforter up around them both and tried not to think about how this woman, so unlike anyone he'd ever met, was worming her way under his skin.

Be careful, a dark little voice warned in his head.

Something about Kat was dangerous. He was feeling things he shouldn't feel, wanting things that hadn't ever mattered before tonight.

I should walk away, but I can't let her go.

৩৩৩

"I NEED YOU TO COME TO THE ADDRESS I'M GOING to text you." Tristan held his mobile close to his ear as he whispered to Carter.

"Bloody hell, Tristan. You realize it's six a.m.? Where the hell are you, anyway, and why do I need to come get you? You took the Aston Martin out. Don't tell me you wrecked it."

Tristan pressed his forehead to the lavatory door in Kat's room.

"I'm at someone's dormitory, but I need trousers. The pair I wore last night met with an accident. Can you get your arse out of bed and meet me here in half an hour?"

Carter's laugh made Tristan squeeze his eyes shut and clench a fist by his head as he sought to quell his temper and humiliation at the reason his trousers had been soiled.

"I think I'll come just to have the pleasure of

seeing you squirm. Text me the address." Carter was still laughing as he hung up.

"Bloody bastard," Tristan muttered as he opened the door and glanced at the bed.

Kat was still asleep, and she looked kissable, fuckable. Perfect in every way a woman could be. The palest of light, more blue than white, filtered through the blinds, stretching across her dormitory windows to illuminate one side of her face and a bare forearm that had slipped free of the covers.

Tristan was captivated by the sight of her. He approached the bed, careful not to wake her. He hadn't ever stayed with a woman past dawn. He'd always slipped out before now, waiting just long enough for his partner to fall asleep before he made his disappearance. But with Kat, he'd fallen asleep himself, deeply, while holding her. He'd been so relaxed, not even an explosion could've woken him. When had sleep ever been that easy? Not in a long while.

Kat shifted, nuzzling her pillow and sighing. The sound sent a blazing path of desire straight to his cock. Tristan forced his eyes away from her and onto his phone, where he texted Kat's dorm information to Carter.

While he waited for Carter to arrive, he studied her room, the books on her shelf by the door, the small, worn collection of travel guides, each one tabbed and highlighted.

She'd lived quite the nomadic life with her father. What had she said? They'd moved every year or so and she'd never known when they'd move again. Something about that made a tightness grow in his chest.

He couldn't get what she'd said last night out of his head. Books didn't leave her, she didn't have to say good-bye.

Tristan took *Dropped from the Clouds* from its box

and wrapped the ribbon around the book. Then with a grin, he placed it on the pillow next to her. It would be there when she woke up.

She hadn't had a chance to look at it last night, but she'd have plenty of time to when he was gone. He wouldn't let her give it back. It was a gift, and if she was going to be spending time with him in bed or out, she'd have to learn to accept the things he bought for her, no matter their price.

The mobile in his hand buzzed with a text from Carter. He was waiting outside.

There was no way he could avoid his friend's teasing. Not when he was practically naked in the dead of winter. Tristan slipped on his sweater and pants from last night and his socks, and then opened Kat's door and crept out into the hallway, where he could see Carter waiting outside the glass door.

His friend was dressed in a gray, knee-length coat and jeans, and he was kicking snow about with one booted foot, his hands shoved into his pockets like an errant schoolboy. A pair of trousers was tucked under one arm.

Tristan unlocked the glass door and pressed a finger to his lips. "Say one bloody word…"

The wicked glint in Carter's eyes assured him that his friend would take full advantage of this situation later.

"Stay out here." He grabbed the trousers and stalked back to Kat's room, leaving Carter out in the cold. When he got back inside her room, he slipped into his new pants and boots. He was in the process of putting his coat on when Kat's voice stopped him.

"You're leaving?" Her sleepy voice filled him with a fuzzy warmth and a desire to stay. But he assumed she had classes most of the day like him, and neither of them could afford to miss them.

He finished putting on his coat and turned to her.

She was sitting up in bed, the covers pooled in her lap. Her hair was sleep mussed and her eyes were soft. She looked like a well-loved woman. Again, that damnable ache flared to life inside him.

Stay. He could see it in her eyes. And it was too dangerous an offer.

"I have an early class." He paused, then strode over to her, putting one knee on the edge of the bed as he leaned over to cup her face in his hands and kiss her. He delved between her startled lips, teasing, nibbling at her mouth, flicking the tip of his tongue against hers, promising her that everything he wanted hadn't faded.

"I want nothing more than to stay right here with you, darling, but we both have things to do today. Shall I drop by tonight?" His tone was...hopeful. Tristan let out a string of curses in his head. Normally he'd just come by and take whatever woman he was seducing right to bed. But not with Kat. Slow seduction, letting her have some control. That was how he'd break down her protective barriers. Then he'd have a chance to set fire to her body with the passion he saw simmering in her eyes.

"Tonight?" She pursed her lips, her eyes hardening a little as she seemed to wake up and consider his proposal.

He brushed his thumbs across her cheeks, praying she'd agree, but then again, it shouldn't matter. He needed to take charge of the situation.

"I'll come by tonight at eight, with dinner." Better to tell her, then let her decide. He grinned at the little frown that creased her brow.

"But—"

He silenced her with another kiss, one just as deep, reminding her with his tongue what he'd done to her with his hand.

She moaned against his lips.

That was how he left her, dazed and dreamy-eyed.

As he exited the dorm, Carter was still outside, arms crossed and grinning a jackal's grin.

"Are you going to tell me about her?" Carter strolled beside him as they made their way down the snow-covered path that cut through the college's main courtyard.

"No. This one is off limits, even for you. I don't want the paparazzi to get wind of her." A shudder rolled through him at the memory of the last woman he'd slept with.

She'd been the daughter of a knighted gentleman out of Surrey, and when the papers had heard of their affair, the pictures of them had been everywhere. Some bastard with a camera had haunted their every step, and the articles hadn't painted their relationship in a flattering light. The relationship hadn't even been serious, a mere fling, but the paparazzi had run with the story for weeks.

His father had been outraged by the situation, and he'd suffered backlash personally as a result. He hadn't approved of the relationship. Not that Tristan had cared because it hadn't been a *real* relationship.

Tristan didn't want his father hearing about Kat for many reasons, but primarily to protect her. His father would find a way to hurt her. He might use his connections to get her thrown out of Cambridge. Or worse, if he thought Kat was in the way of his plans for Tristan to marry a woman he believed more suitable for the Countess of Pembroke title.

Like Brianna Wolverton. She was the daughter of a viscount his father had known for years. Tristan had a tendency to hook up with her on occasion, to scratch a mutual itch they both had. He and Brianna had been in the press more often than Prince Harry and Prince William. So much so that they were often considered a celebrity couple despite Tristan's every attempt to declare otherwise. Brianna had no desire or expectations of any relationship either, but the papers loved to gossip about them.

"Are you worried about the paparazzi or your father?" Carter asked. His friend knew first-hand what a brute the Earl of Pembroke could be, particularly when voicing his opinions on social status.

"Both. Father won't find out unless the paps do." They passed through the archway to the college entrance and out onto the street. Each step he took away from Kat left a hollow sensation in his chest.

"Celia texted me about some party." Carter interrupted Tristan's brooding.

"Yes. I told her you'd be happy to help arrange it." Tristan chuckled as his friend gaped at him.

"A party? At Fox Hill? It's not exactly a prime location."

"I know. I want to have a few particular individuals attend."

"Your new girl, you mean. Why? Didn't you sleep with her last night? You rarely go back to a woman for seconds."

"*Sleep* is the operative word. She's...not the sort of girl you sleep with on the first night." He and Carter shared almost everything, but Kat was something he wanted to keep secret.

"Let me make sure I understand this." Carter was laughing again.

The bastard.

"*You* are interested in a woman who actually needs to be wooed? Are you feeling well?" He snickered.

Tristan ground his teeth. Although his past liaisons were with more worldly women, that didn't mean he couldn't be interested a woman like Kat.

"Tristan." Carter sobered. "If you are chasing this poor girl because she's shiny, new, and a challenge, that's not very noble."

"Since when have I ever been noble?" Tristan shot back, his temper flaring.

Carter shook his head. "Come to think of it, never. I've seen you take two women to bed at one time."

Tristan smiled. "That was a fun night. We need to do something like that again. It's been too long." He had no intention of sleeping with anyone but Kat in the near future, but he'd never let Carter know just how affected he was by her. It was a vulnerability he was still trying to understand, and having Carter poke fun at him for it didn't sound appealing.

His friend rolled his eyes. "It was last month."

"Exactly my point."

"You're a damned libertine, you know that?" Carter chuckled.

"Maybe I am." Tristan was already feeling better.

Now if he could only get Kat in his bed...naked, without any of her worries, he'd prove to her how hot things could get between them. He'd prove it all night and clear through till morning, and she would love every minute of it.

❧ 11 ❧

A violent wave of nausea rolled through Kat as she stared at the newspaper. Her world, so carefully constructed to protect her from everything, was now crumbling around her. Ripples of an emotional aftershock rocked through her and her limbs quaked. The paper crinkled as she clenched her fists and blinked back tears.

The newspaper had been lying on her study table, abandoned by some reader before she and Lacy had come to the library to study. As they'd settled in, something on the front page had caught her eye.

The image knocked the breath from her lungs.

There it was. A grainy, black-and-white photo of a man and a woman in the back of a pub. The man had the woman pinned against the wall, one hand sliding up the outside of her skirt. Their mouths were locked in a deep kiss.

She recognized the dominant way the man captured the woman in his arms, his possessive hands roaming over her. It was all too familiar. Once she saw his face, those awful rumblings deep inside her soul had started.

It was Tristan. Kissing another woman. When had he found the time to go be with another woman? Did it matter? He *had* somehow, and Kat felt like an idiot because she'd known from the start that he was a womanizer.

*But I wanted him to be different with me...*And that only made her feel more stupid. *Hope*. Hope that she'd be special to him, and she hadn't been.

"It's him, isn't it?" Lacy said. She pushed her hair over one shoulder. "Tristan Kingsley."

Kat's throat constricted and she swallowed hard. All she could see was Tristan with some woman...his hands...touching that woman like he'd touched her last night. Intimately.

"This could be an old picture," Lacy said as she pried the newspaper from her hands. "He's always in the papers."

"That's just it," Kat whispered. "Even if it is old... look at him...It's so public and...what if he meets another girl today before he sees me and he loses interest...?" There was nothing tying him to her, so why had she been so foolish as to think she could lay any claim to him?

Last night with him had been so amazing and everything between them had been intense. She'd felt connected to him in so many ways.

Now I'm the fool. Because it was probably all one-sided, no matter what he said. It's just a game to him.

"I...think I'm gonna be sick." She leapt up from the table at the library and bolted for the bathroom.

She barricaded herself in a stall and leaned against the door, trying to avoid throwing up. The cool metal of the stall almost burned her bare hands when she pressed them flat on the door. Her pulse pounded through her with the force of timpani drums, drowning out all other sounds around her.

Last night had been wonderful. *Tristan* had been wonderful.

It was all a lie.

She was just a pawn in a game he was playing.

Pain lanced through her heart, and she sucked in a gasping breath.

The arrogant asshole had convinced her to open up to him, to reveal vulnerable parts of herself she hadn't wanted to share.

The picture told her everything she knew about Tristan but had ignored.

He was bad news. Dangerous.

She'd knowingly played with fire and gotten burned.

I thought the thing between us was special. But it's not. I'm just like every other girl to him.

She couldn't hate him. She'd gone into this with her eyes wide open, but her heart had been open too. He was irresistible.

His swagger, that cocky grin, the way he'd simply held her as they'd slept together. As if he'd *known* he could manipulate her so easily. *And wasn't I the fool for letting him do that to me.*

"Kat?" Lacy's voice interrupted her inner tirade. "You in here?"

Wiping her eyes, she sucked in a few deep breaths before she answered. "I'm here." She left the stall and saw Lacy leaning back against the sink, arms crossed, mouth thinned into a firm line with worry.

"I'm so sorry, Kat." Lacy uncrossed her arms and hugged Kat tight.

Kat sunk into Lacy's embrace, needing the comfort Lacy offered.

"It's okay." She sniffed, hating that a *man* had made her cry. "I was dumb enough to think he'd be different with me. I guess every girl thinks that, huh?"

Her friend shrugged. "It happens. We all think we're different." Lacy paused. "I do think that picture is old, though. You've only known him a few days. Maybe it will be different for you?" The question in

Lacy's tone didn't make the anxious knot in Kat's stomach disappear.

"What's that saying about a leopard and spots?" Her chuckle was watery. "I should have realized he won't be the kind of guy who changes. If he's used to having a lot of women around, I doubt he'll change for me." *Because I'm a nobody*...That thought was icy cold and depressing. She wasn't anyone a future earl would care about. She didn't have an aristocratic pedigree, didn't have estates and titles...there was nothing special about her that would entice Tristan to give her another thought.

"Stupid men." Lacy echoed her thoughts. "Mark could rough him up. He would, you know."

Kat shook her head. "No. He isn't worth the time Mark would waste pounding his face into a wall."

"True," Lacy agreed. "But it'd make me feel better."

"Yeah." She didn't want to hurt Tristan, even though he'd hurt her. Vengeance wouldn't ease the soreness in her heart.

When she got hurt, she ran, hid, refused to lash out. It was a trait she'd inherited from her father. He'd been running away every day since her mother had left.

"Lacy, he said he was coming to my place tonight. I can't be there. Can we do something? Go out, see a movie. *Something*," Kat begged. If she couldn't find a distraction, she was going to lose it, *bad*.

Lacy's face wilted. "I wish I could. Got a paper due in my American literature class. Mark's free. Want me to text him?"

"Could you?" Kat lunged for that life raft, clinging to it.

Her friend tapped furiously on her phone as she sent Mark a message. A second later her phone chimed, and Lacy grinned.

"He's happy to do it, but he says you have to go to a pub with him. American football is on tonight and he wants to watch it." Lacy made a goofy face that had Kat giggling. Lacy didn't understand the sport, and her boyfriend's obsession with it made just as little sense to her.

"Perfect. I'll be distracted."

"Good, now that we've got that settled, we should get back to studying." Lacy linked her arm through Kat's.

Her cell phone vibrated in her pocket, and her dad's picture flashed across the screen.

"Lacy, can you watch my stuff? My dad's calling."

"Of course," Lacy said.

Kat hastily ducked outside the study rooms and into the hall, where she answered, her voice still a little shaky from crying. "Hey, Dad, what's up?"

"Hey, honey. I was wondering if you had a minute to talk?" She resisted the instant pang of homesickness as she heard her father's deep voice. London was far enough away that she missed him. It was the first time in her life she was really living apart from him.

"Sure, Dad. I was just studying with Lacy. What's up?"

There was a heartbeat of a pause before he spoke.

"It's...well..." He exhaled and her heart jolted.

"What is it? Did something happen to Mom?" It was one of her deepest fears—even though she hadn't heard from her in years. The occasional birthday card was Kat's only assurance that her mother hadn't died. But that didn't stop Kat from keeping a few faded photographs of her mother tucked away in her books and looking at them occasionally.

As much as she hated that her mother had run out on her and her father, she missed having a mother, another woman in her life.

Her father cleared his throat. "As far as I know,

your mother is fine." He paused, then coughed again. "What I have to say has something to do with me and your mother, sort of..."

Kat knew that tone well enough, and she could almost see him grimace.

"Dad, please, just tell me," she whispered, her heart hammering hard enough to bruise her ribs.

"I've been dating someone for the last two months. A woman I met in London. I kept things casual, and I haven't told you before now because it wasn't serious. But now, well, it's serious," he said. "I wouldn't have dropped this on you right before exams, but you're coming straight to London after your tests, and you'll be meeting her over the holidays. I thought you could use the winter break to meet her."

Kat struggled to breathe. She'd given up long ago on the idea that her mother would ever come back; she wasn't that foolish. Over the years she'd gotten used to having her father to herself. He was always there when she called and ready to drop everything for her. What would happen when he had someone else to care for?

Yet...he deserved to move on, to be happy. What kind of daughter was she if she wouldn't want that for him? She took a few deep breaths.

"Okay...what's she like?" Her knuckles whitened with her death grip on her phone.

"She's wonderful, Kat. Smart, beautiful, compassionate. She's divorced, too, and has a son about your age, maybe a little older. Her name is Lizzy. We were thinking it might be nice to celebrate the holidays together, the four of us. You'd get to meet her and her son."

Kat didn't say anything.

Clearing his throat again, her father continued. "What do you think? I know it's bad timing with your exams, but I've been spending a lot of time at her place, instead of my flat. I really want you two to meet because I'm crazy about her." Her father's tone was hesitant but also hopeful. How could she say no?

"That sounds...great, Dad. I can't wait to meet them." Tears pricked the corners of her eyes. He was spending a lot of time at this woman's place? He really *was* serious about her...Little jolts of pain stung her heart.

"I love her, Kat. Lizzy makes me happy."

Kat could hear the affection in his voice, and strangely, it made the ache in her chest ease. Her father was excited, in love, and she realized she wanted that for him more than anything.

"How did you meet her?" Relaxing, she leaned back against the wall as she listened to him describe their first meeting at a grocery store.

"I broke an entire carton of eggs right on her shoes. She dropped a melon on mine. We made such a mess, crashing into each other like that. We started talking as we helped clean up and one thing led to another. I asked her out. I still can't believe she agreed." He chuckled, then grew serious again. "We've both been through hell with our previous spouses. Being a single parent isn't easy. It's lonely. When I met her, something just clicked."

"I'm so happy for you, Dad." Kat swallowed past the lump in her throat. It was stupid and irrational, but she felt like she was being orphaned. If he had Lizzy, then he might spend less time with her, and she'd be more alone than ever.

"Honey," her father said, sighing, "I've sprung this on you with no warning. I'm sorry."

"It's fine. Really." Shuffling one boot on the floor, she drew patterns in the carpet.

"No." Her father's voice became firm. "You know that nothing in this world changes how I feel about you. There is no competition between you and anyone I become involved with. Tell me you believe me."

Kat bit her lip. She'd never had a frank discussion about this with her father, not about something so... personal and awkward. She shuddered, holding in a shaky breath.

"I know, Dad."

"Good." He changed his tone, lightening up. "When you come to London, we'll stay at Lizzy's home. She has a wonderful town house, three stories. Plenty of room for you, me, and Lizzy's son."

What? Stay at her dad's girlfriend's house? That sounded horrible, cramped in a flat over Christmas with her dad, his girlfriend, and her son. But she could do it for him. *Yeah*...She rubbed her closed eyes. "Sounds great!" she said, hiding her sadness beneath a falsely cheery tone.

"All right, honey. I'll let you get back to studying."

"Thanks. Love you, Dad."

"Love you too, sweetie."

Kat disconnected and slipped the phone into her jeans pocket before going into the library again.

Lacy perked up when she saw Kat. "Everything okay with your dad?"

"Yeah. He met someone, and they're pretty serious. He wants me to spend Christmas with them."

"'Them'?" Her friend closed the textbook and then propped her elbows on it, fully focusing on Kat.

"His girlfriend has a son. Around my age, or a little older."

"Oh, really? Is he cute?"

An exasperated laugh escaped Kat. "Seriously? Lacy, I don't know anything about him, and I wasn't about to ask my dad." *Not to mention, my world is imploding, and cute guys are the last thing on my mind.* "Just finish your homework," she said, tapping Lacy's book.

"Boo!" Lacy muttered, but she flipped open her textbook again, sighing dramatically.

"The quicker we finish our reading, the quicker we can leave. I've got to meet Mark in two hours," Kat said.

Lacy rolled her eyes and mumbled something about Kat being an evil taskmaster before she settled in to study.

Kat, however, couldn't focus. Between Tristan's photo in the tabloids and her dad's new girlfriend, studying was going to be impossible.

The library door opened, and a man walked in. Tall, fair-haired, and gorgeous, he looked to be in his mid-twenties. The gray trousers and elegant black coat he wore made him look too sexy for the library. He reminded her of Tristan, in the way he moved with lithe grace and a slight swagger that suggested a woman wouldn't be able to resist sleeping with him.

"Oh, hello, handsome." Lacy stifled a giggle.

"You have a boyfriend," Kat chastised, but she was grinning.

"Yeah," Lacy scoffed. "I love him to death, but that doesn't mean I can't appreciate a beautiful man when I see one."

They watched the man walk from table to table in the library, handing out little cards to people, smiling and chatting before moving on. Finally, he reached them.

Lacy nudged Kat underneath the table with her foot.

With a wince, Kat rubbed her legs together, trying to soothe the stinging spot on her right shin.

"Good afternoon, ladies," he said, his British accent smooth as music. Just like Tristan's. *Damn*, she had to stop thinking about him or she'd go crazy.

"I'm having a celebration in two weeks for the end of exams. Magdalene College students only. If you're interested, here's the address." He slid two silver cards along their reading table with a finger.

"We're not really the party—" Kat began but was cut off when a sharp elbow jabbed her ribs. She coughed violently.

"Thank you. We'll be there." Lacy smiled up at the man. "What's your name?"

"Carter Martin." The man smiled, his expression filled with promise as he winked and turned away.

"Lacy, what the hell? I'm not going to that party." Kat kept one palm flat on her side where her ribs ached from Lacy's elbow.

With a delicate flourish, Lacy held up the silver card. "Did you see the address? The party's at one of those expensive houses on the hill. Beautiful and built with old money. You'll love it. Trust me, we can go for half an hour, then leave if you want."

Kat glanced at the silver card. The date was a week from Friday. Final exams would be over. Nibbling her lip, she debated. What could it hurt? She loved older houses, especially around Cambridge.

"Fine. But if it's not fun, I'm leaving."

"Deal." Lacy claimed the second silver card for herself. "This will be fun."

❧ 12 ❧

Tristan hummed as he walked to Kat's dorm. It was eight o'clock, and she'd be expecting him for dinner.

Tonight...he was going to take everything further, show Kat she could trust him enough to sleep with him, because he couldn't last another night in bed beside her without making love to her. He'd spent the entire day thinking about her, about how they'd spent the night, how it had felt to hold her and talk about things he'd never shared with anyone. He wanted more of that, more of Kat.

When he reached her room he knocked, grinning. There was a lightness and a fluttering excitement inside him. It had been years since chasing a woman had been this invigorating. She played with him, teased him back, made him enjoy this courtship dance.

Kat didn't come to the door. Frowning, he pounded on the wood again with a balled fist.

Still silence.

"Kat? It's me. I have dinner," he called out. She had to hear him. He smacked a fist on her door and growled. Bloody idiot that he was, he didn't have her mobile number.

"Kat!"

Still that awful, heavy silence.

Then the door at the end of the hall opened, and a young woman peered out of her door. She looked vaguely familiar, and he wondered where he might have seen her before.

"She's not here," the girl said. Blonde hair spilled around her shoulders, and she wore warm-looking pajamas. Another undergraduate studying hard for exams. Judging by the firm line of her lips and her hands resting on her hips, he'd clearly disturbed her.

Tristan set the food down by the door. "Do you know where Kat is?"

"You're Tristan Kingsley, aren't you?" the girl said, completely ignoring his question.

Something twisted in his stomach, making him feel ill. It never went well when someone recognized him. He'd managed to keep a fairly low profile since his return to Cambridge for the Master's program, and he'd hate for that to change and have the paps hounding him on school grounds.

"And if I am?"

The girl opened the door wider so she faced him head on, arms crossed.

"Then I'll tell you to leave. She doesn't want to see you anymore." The finality of the girl's tone hit him hard enough to knock the wind out of him.

"Wh—what?"

"She saw a photo of you in the paper with another woman. She won't date someone like you. So you might as well leave." The girl's scowl could've frozen the surface of the sun.

"The paper?" *Fucking hell.* That damned photo from last week was going to haunt him forever.

"I'll explain that photo to her, but I'm not leaving. I'll wait here all night if I have to." He leaned against the wall by Kat's door, making a show of settling in.

The girl's frown only deepened. "Suit yourself, but she's moved on from you." Then she slipped back into her room and closed the door, leaving him to brood and ponder on his own.

Moved on from me?

No woman had ever walked away from him. *No one.* He'd always been the one to end to things. He'd be damned if he'd let Kat just leave him like this over a damned photo taken weeks before he'd met her. It wasn't just his pride...There was so much more he'd wanted to do with her...not just physically. He'd loved talking to her, being around her, making her laugh...It had felt so bloody good just being with her. And now she was trying to reject that? Reject him?

I'll be damned if I let that happen.

The minutes ticked by. Tristan ended up sitting on the floor against her door, resting his arms on one raised knee. The food had long since gone cold, and his mood had soured as well, but he'd wait all night to talk to her.

The main dormitory door clicked as it opened and people began coming down the hall, just out of sight. Tristan scrambled to his feet, dusting his coat and pants off. Kat and a man came around the corner, but she skidded to a halt when she saw him. The man behind her bumped into her back and steadied himself by gripping her waist with his hands.

A veil of red descended over Tristan's vision, and he lunged for the other man, shoving him hard enough that he stumbled back, hitting the wall.

"Tristan! What are you doing? Stop it!" Kat turned her back on Tristan to speak to the other man. "Are you okay, Mark?"

Mark blinked, apparently stunned, then shook his head, straightened, and raised his fists.

"You want to fight? I'd be happy to oblige, you bleeding sod," he growled.

"Bring it on, I was a boxing champ during university." Tristan grabbed Kat. She didn't fight him when he moved her behind him. Then he lifted his fists.

"Sounds good to me." Mark stepped closer and the pair of them squared off.

Kat darted out and wedged herself between them, a hand on each of their chests, forcing them back.

"Cut it out! Both of you!" she snapped.

"Kat, who is he?" Tristan demanded, breathing hard. Blood roared in his ears as he fought to calm down. There was no way she was seeing this man, not after what they'd shared the night before. The thought of her with someone else after he'd exposed his soul to her made him sick to his stomach. He was not about to lose her to this fool, whoever he was.

"Mark is a friend." Her hand on his chest rubbed him slightly. He doubted she was even aware that she was doing it. It soothed him, but only just.

"I've been waiting here for two hours." Tristan's voice had a cold edge to it, which reminded him of his father. He kept his eyes on Mark.

The man still had his fists half-raised. "I can take him, Kat, just give me the go-ahead."

Kat made a small growl. "No! No more fighting. Mark, go to Lacy's room. I'll be fine. Tristan and I have to talk."

Mark hesitated. "Are you sure? I'd be happy to summon the porter and have him throw this sod out."

"You'll behave, won't you?" Kat asked Tristan, but it sounded more like a command.

He frowned at her, not liking that she was giving him orders, but for her, he'd agree. Her brows were drawn together and her lips pursed in a tight line. He wanted her smiling, or laughing breathlessly, not this anxious, pale-faced woman who stared at him now. Something about seeing her distressed made his pulse race and his muscles tense.

"I'll behave," he muttered, shoving his hands into his coat pockets.

"Okay." Kat exhaled, her shoulders dropping. She gave a gentle shove to Mark's chest. "Go to Lacy."

Mark finally walked down the hall, knocked on the door there, and the blonde woman re-appeared in the doorway. So that was Lacy?

Lacy's eyes widened when she saw Tristan and Kat.

"Kat, are you okay?" Even though the question was directed at Kat, Lacy's eyes settled on him, and a look he knew all too well was shot his way. One that said, "You hurt my friend, I'll castrate you." At any other time it would have delighted him to know that Kat had such loyal and protective friends, but not when said friends were attempting to keep him away from his woman.

Mark leaned in to Lacy, whispering something in her ear as his hands settled on her waist. Tristan watched him, strangely jealous of their open intimacy. He wanted to hold Kat the same way, have that same familiarity and right to touch her like a man in a relationship could.

Kat unlocked her door and turned to face him. Distrust and anger shadowed her lovely eyes.

Seeing that made him want to punch a wall. Hard.

He gathered the bag of cold French cuisine from the floor and followed her inside, closing the door with one foot. For a moment he struggled, words unable to form as he fought the urge to drag her into his arms and kiss all protests off her lips.

When her gaze dropped to the bag of food in his arms, he almost sighed in relief. *Dinner*, that was a word he could get out. Much safer than to admit his pride was wounded at her standing him up. Well, fucking hell, it was more than just his hurt pride, but he wouldn't dare admit that particular weakness.

"Kat, I told you I'd be here for dinner tonight."

She blew out a breath and faced him. A sinking feeling swept through him as he saw a decisive look carved into her delicate features.

"Tristan, we can't do this. I'm sorry," she said, maintaining a distance between them.

It seemed as if an ocean separated them. If he could just grasp her, draw her close and remind her of the electricity that sparked every time they touched, she wouldn't be able to push him away, but her words rooted his feet to the ground.

"No. We haven't even begun. You cannot shut me out."

She lifted her chin. "Lacy warned me about what kind of man you were, but I didn't want to believe her. I gave you a chance, but she was right. I was stupid to think you'd be different with me."

"So you judge me without explanation?" He didn't recognize his own voice. His words were dragged out of him, low and rough.

The food bag dropped to the ground with a thunderous smack. He stepped forward, leaning in close.

She stumbled in retreat, falling flat on her delectable ass when the backs of her knees hit the bed. Her eyes, wide with fright and inner pain, shined up at him, making him feel every inch the villain as he towered over to her.

"Kat, let me explain." He eased down on one knee in front of her, putting them eye-to-eye. When he reached for her hands, she tugged them away, and the action burned him to the core.

A heavy silence settled between them and was only broken when she finally moved and pulled out a newspaper from beneath a pillow on her bed. She slapped it against his chest and crossed her arms.

Tristan stared at the picture of him and Brianna.

"This isn't okay. Not for me. I won't be with a guy,

let alone sleep with him, when he's doing this with another woman."

The pages crinkled as his hands clenched.

Have to calm down. He let go of the newspaper. He could explain this and she'd forgive him because he hadn't been with anyone since meeting her. More importantly, he didn't *want* anyone but her.

"That was taken two weeks ago, before I met you. Her name is Brianna. She and I have— had an understanding. Until I met you..."

Kat scoffed, but he didn't miss the pain in her voice, and it sliced him deep with an invisible blade.

"An understanding? What does that even mean?"

Tristan raked a hand through his hair, facing her.

"She and I have seen each other on and off for years. She's never wanted a relationship, and neither have I. It's been more to scratch an itch than anything." For the first time in his life he wished he had never slept with Brianna.

"You mean like friends with benefits?" Kat asked, staring at the picture, her eyes still glimmering with tears. He got up from his knee and sat on the bed beside her.

"That's a very American way to put it, but yes. I haven't seen her since that photo was taken two weeks ago. And since I met you two days ago, there hasn't been anyone else." He reached for one of her hands again, but she shrank away. His empty palm dropped to the bed between them.

He tried to breathe, but it felt like a boulder was crushing his chest.

"So you'll judge me for something I did before I met you? I never professed to be a bloody saint!" Anger prickled beneath his skin, and he struggled to keep the dangerous edge out of his voice.

She blinked. "I don't know," she admitted. "We haven't even known each other a week."

"Then give this a chance, Kat!" His voice rose, and he got to his feet, but he forced his hands to stay at his sides. If he didn't, he'd touch her, and he couldn't promise not to kiss her, to remind her that what they felt for each other couldn't be denied.

"No! I can't date a man who will likely cheat on me as soon as he gets bored. I have more respect for myself than that." She got off her bed and walked to her desk, slapping her palms down on her textbooks. Her head bowed slightly.

"I'd never cheat on you. Bloody hell, woman, I swear on my life, *on my title*, I would not." How could she accuse him of something like that? She'd never given him a chance to prove he wouldn't.

Her head lifted, and she looked at him, those gray eyes burning through him.

"You think I'll agree to sleep with you because you're going to be an earl? I don't give a damn about that. You seem to think it matters that you're going to be powerful someday. You can have any woman you want, but not me. I don't need to get my heart broken by you. I'm not willing to take that chance."

The finality in her tone broke him in two.

Nothing had ever done that. Why the bloody hell did she matter so much? He had never felt the compulsion to become obsessed with a woman, so why did he feel like he couldn't let her walk out of his life?

He wanted to shake her, grasp her shoulders and rattle her until she got her senses back. When he raised his hands, she lifted her chin. That defiance made him furious and desperate to kiss her. But she wouldn't let him.

Tristan stared at the floor for a long moment. Inside, everything was spinning. Outside, he remained cool and calm as he'd always done when life seemed determined to crush him. Echoes from his past, his father's cruelty, his mother's hurt rumbled from deep inside, where he'd buried them.

I cannot let those old wounds reopen.

Somehow he found the strength to stand, his fists clenching and unclenching at his sides as he collected himself.

"There is something between us, something deep and powerful, and you're going to let it go?" How could she not feel this intense pull? Sure, it was bloody well terrifying to admit he felt it, but he did. He didn't want to ignore it, not when everything about being with her felt so right. The thought that he'd never see her again choked him.

"It's not worth the risk." Her voice was hollow. But tears streamed down her cheeks. She didn't want to admit it, but she was hurting as much as he was.

So be it.

"Fine. I'll leave you alone, if that's what you really want." He slowly rose from her bed, grabbed his bag of food from the floor, and walked to the door.

"Have a nice life, Katherine." He meant it, even though there was a bitter taste in his mouth and an odd ache in his chest.

"Tristan…" His name was a soft plea, but it wasn't enough.

He stepped outside and closed the door, hating her, hating himself, yet he wanted to go back in there and kiss her until he destroyed her foolish idea of resisting him. If he had the chance to get her flat on her bed, he would kiss every inch of her, convince her he was loyal, and that he didn't want anyone but her. He'd never wanted just one woman before, but Kat was different. What they had was different. And she'd ruined everything because she wouldn't trust him.

It's too late. Too bloody late.

Kat wiped away her tears. Letting Tristan walk out the door and not running after him had cut her in two. He'd taken half of her with him, and she was terrified of what that meant. She couldn't fall for him, and shouldn't feel so devastated because she'd let him break through her carefully constructed walls. The moment he had shut the door between them it had shattered her, and yet she was the one who'd demanded he leave.

How can I feel this way about someone I've only known a few days?

It didn't make sense. She couldn't forget what he'd said. There was something connecting them, something she couldn't explain but could feel. Was it just wild, insane lust or was it something deeper? Now that it was over, how was she going to get through this?

She was definitely not okay, but that was her own fault. She'd let Tristan walk away before she'd had time to figure out what she really wanted. And she'd never given him the chance to explain. Her pride had gotten in the way, and she'd just shut him out to protect herself. It hadn't worked. She felt like she was bleeding inside.

She collapsed on the bed, and the tears came. Between fighting with Tristan and her father dating someone, it seemed her entire world was crumbling around her. Everything was changing too quickly.

Kat wasn't sure how long she cried, but at some point she slipped into sleep.

She dreamed about a house on a hill, with snow-capped chimneys and ice lacing the edges of the windows. It was a place of dreams and fairy tales, with magic emanating from the snow-covered grounds. A sleek, red fox padded around softly in the gardens outside, sniffing the air before vanishing into the nearest hedge.

A solitary figure in the window paced back and forth. She recognized the man with dark hair and blue-green eyes that burned like stars in a clear night sky. For a brief time, this beautiful man had been hers, and for one night they'd shared passions, dreams, and whispered confessions of the heart.

Tristan. The window around the Tristan of her dream shattered. Kat jerked awake with a gasp. Her heart beat so hard she could barely think. Blood roared in her ears, making her dizzy.

She was alone in her dorm room. Tristan and the beautiful snowy house on the hill were a dream. Nothing more.

She turned on the lamp and reached for her laptop on the nightstand. She pulled up an Internet search for Tristan Kingsley. She hadn't wanted to see evidence of his past, not after the first time she and Lacy had Googled him. But now she *needed* to see it. Plenty of tabloid pictures, usually of Tristan and some woman dancing at a club, drinking at a bar, or dining at a restaurant. Most of the time he was with that girl, Brianna. Every time Kat came across an article, it never failed to mention Tristan's father, the Earl of Pembroke, and the earl's current political power plays.

Why would all of the articles attempt to use Tristan's playboy character against his father's public image? Unless...that was their intention. Use the son to discredit the father.

Kat remembered Tristan's face, the way his eyes had hardened, the way his jaw had tensed when he'd spoken about his father. Their relationship must be strained, and it no doubt wasn't helped by this type of article.

Kat perused the articles again, reading over everything, studying Tristan's posture and attitude in the photos. Aside from the extremely risqué picture with his hand up Brianna's skirt, there wasn't much in the way of bad behavior. No assaults, no drugs, no drunkenness. Just scores of women and the scandal of his libertine lifestyle. A typical playboy. But not really a bad guy.

Tristan said he hadn't been with anyone since he'd met her. They'd only known each other two days, and she'd known at the back of her mind that he couldn't have been with anyone else that quickly. Yet she'd judged him anyway. He'd wanted to give whatever was between them a chance, and she'd shut him down so fast they'd failed to get anywhere.

Am I that afraid of a photograph of him and some other woman taken before he met me?

She was, and she hated that she was so scared of getting hurt. He'd been right. She was young and she should be living and having fun, not locking herself away from anything that might hurt her later. Wasn't falling in love and dating part of that?

I had an adventure right there and I shoved him out the door. And now I can't even contact him to...to what? Talk? Go out on a real date? Tell him I want him and that I'm ready to risk my heart to be with him?

She had no phone number or e-mail address—nothing. He was at a different college within the university. Their paths might never cross again. Not to mention, she'd burned her bridges when they'd fought, and he wouldn't forgive her. She couldn't forgive herself for stopping something before they'd had a chance to start.

I'll never know what it would have been like to be with him.

She closed the laptop and set it aside, a hollowness growing inside her chest until bleak despair covered her like a suffocating shroud.

What have I done?

❧ 13 ❧

The past two weeks had been hell. *Beyond hell*. Tristan hadn't bothered to shave for a week. He'd barely managed to shower and stumble into his classes. Carter had threatened to shove him out on his arse in the snow if he didn't clean up for the party tonight.

But none of it mattered. Kat had shut him out of her life. The spark of something deep and hot between them had been buried by her closing the door that night. The finality of her decision had ripped through him so hard he'd been unable to drive for several minutes after leaving her dormitory. Instead, he'd wandered the snowy grounds, hands shoved deep into his pockets, his mind trying to sort through the pain and the anger over her rejection. When he'd finally come home that night, he'd poured every bit of his soul into the nearest glass of brandy and hadn't come out of the bottle since.

"You look like bloody hell," Carter mused from the doorway. His smug grin made Tristan growl and clench his fists around the soft towel as he wiped his face dry. He'd showered and dressed in a pair of jeans. Their house would be full of people tonight, but he was tempted to go downstairs as he was. That would certainly be scandalous. He felt reckless enough that he just might do it. What was one more scandal in the papers? His father would be furious, but what else was new?

"The razor is within reach, Carter. I'd watch your words," he warned.

"As if you could do anything. I've watched you drink yourself into the bottom of your mother's most expensive Scotch this week. I dare you to throw a decent punch."

"You're one to talk. Celia's come around four times, and you duck and run."

Carter's mouth thinned into a scowl. "We both know why I avoid her."

Tristan tossed the towel onto the counter, glowering at his friend in the mirror's reflection.

"Don't you have a party to host with Celia?"

"Only because you won't come down and join us. We got this together for you, and you aren't even attending."

Well played. Tristan scrubbed a hand over his chin. He'd gotten his friend and cousin into this party all because he'd hoped it would be one more way to woo Kat. If she loved Fox Hill he'd be that much closer to winning her over. And it had all been a wasted effort, because she would never want him again, would never trust him over things he'd done before he'd met her.

Life up until now had been a loving mistress to him. Now she was a cold-hearted creature digging her claws into his chest. The one thing he wanted most in the world...Kat...was something he couldn't have.

"Are you really not going to come down to the party?" Carter asked.

Exhaling, Tristan rubbed his temples, trying to ease the throb of a building headache. "The whole point of tonight's festivities no longer exists for me."

Carter's irritation changed to sympathy. "Are you

certain? I handed out dozens of invitations to undergraduate students. How do you know she won't come?"

"She's not the party type. I was hoping to entice her to come before..." *Before she ripped me in two.*

His friend pushed away from the door frame and sighed. "I'm sorry, Tristan. Wherever the girl is, she's twisted you up in knots. I suggest you sort yourself out before we go on holiday. Your mother won't want her time with you to be—" he waved a hand up and down at Tristan's body "—like this. She deserves her son to be on his best behavior."

Best behavior? Had he *ever* behaved? No, and he had no intention of starting now.

"Get out of my room, Carter, and go downstairs to keep Celia company."

His friend shrugged and then left.

Tristan could hear the low bass of music downstairs, that blend of chatter and laughter unique only to parties. Since Celia was in charge, it was more upscale than a typical university party. They were also past that wild stage of partying that came with the newly minted college students.

Drunken escapades had lost their appeal after he'd turned twenty-two. Now he preferred his parties on the quiet side, with drinks and entertainment of a more private nature, preferably in a bed. He would have none of that tonight. Kat should have been here. He'd planned to show her the house, tell her its history, seduce her with the things she loved most and prove to her that he cared about her. Because he *did*, he cared too bloody much, and all it had gotten him was pain.

Why the hell did it hurt so much not having her here? She was just a girl, wasn't she? He'd had plenty of them over the years...so why did Kat matter? Why couldn't he get the thought of her mercury gray eyes out of his head, or the sound of her laugh out of his ears? His hands trembled with longing for her, to touch her, thread his fingers through her silky hair. He missed everything about her.

Fuck. This was going to be a long night.

He slipped out of the bathroom and moved through the darkened bedroom to his closet. The cold weather outside wasn't going to matter, not with all the people flooding Fox Hill, so Tristan opted for a black T-shirt rather than a sweater.

Tugging the shirt over his head, he padded to the wide window and shoved one curtain back to peer through the frosted glass. Below him, the main driveway was full of cars. Headlights from some of the newer arrivals burned bright in the night, cutting through the heavily falling snow, creating gold beams that glowed with an ethereal luminescence.

He watched the snow fall for several minutes, his thoughts as scattered as the falling flakes outside, until his mobile rang. He had no intention of answering, but when he saw the caller ID he changed his mind.

"Mum?"

"Hello, Tristan, dear."

He loved the sound of her voice, sweet and kind, full of affection for him. So different from his father's.

"Am I still due to come stay with you in two days?" He hoped she hadn't changed her plans. The last thing he wanted was to end up with his father on holiday. The arrogant man already thought Tristan was coming and would be furious when he discovered his son had lied.

"Yes." Her breathless reply was quick. "But I want to talk to you."

He continued to stare out the window as he waited for her to speak.

"I've met someone, Tristan. A wonderful man. We've been dating these last few months, and I want you to meet him."

Everything inside him stilled. His mother had met a man? He was happy for her, of course. But he'd make sure that whoever this fellow was, he was good enough for her. His mother was often a target because of her property and her family money. Men without scruples saw her as a way to wealth and power.

The last time his mother had believed she was in love, the man had been a gentleman from a good family who'd gone deep into debt. He'd attempted to seduce her while still married. When his mother had discovered that the man hadn't yet divorced his wife, it had crushed her. Tristan had vowed that wouldn't happen again, not while he was there to watch out for her.

"That's good to hear, Mum. Who is he?"

"He's an investment banker." His mother chuckled. "And no, he has no interest in my money. He has plenty on his own."

Tristan smiled, shaking his head. It was like she'd heard his thoughts. "That's good. How did you meet?" He wasn't thrilled at the idea of a strange man in his mother's life, but he'd attempt to sound happy for her. He would also have the man thoroughly checked out.

His mother launched into an amusing story of running into the man at a grocer.

"We want you to meet. We thought we could stay together over Christmas."

Tristan digested this, pacing as he mulled it over. Given the situation with Kat, he desperately needed a distraction, even one that wouldn't be necessarily positive. He would rather deal with his mother's relationship than his own.

"Is this all right, Tristan? I don't want to upset your holiday. We just thought it would be the best time for all of us to get together."

"It's fine, Mum. I'll be delighted to meet him."

"Wonderful. He has a daughter, a girl near your age. I haven't met her yet, but he says she's a sweet girl."

That made him groan. The last thing he wanted to do was interact with the girl during the holidays.

"Mum, that sounds lovely. Do you mind if I call you tomorrow?"

She laughed. "Of course, darling."

Tristan tossed his mobile on the bed and started toward the door. He needed to get drunk again. *Now.*

❧ 14 ❧

Lacy was right. As usual. Not that Kat would ever admit it.

Mark parked the car at the end of the circular drive, and they stepped out into the snowstorm. Her ankle-high boots and little black dress weren't the best clothes for tramping about in the snow, but at least she had on a thick, black woolen coat, which she clutched tightly around her as she followed her friends. They were teasing each other, knocking their shoulders together while they whispered and laughed.

A pang of pain rang through her, as sharp as a silver bell struck with a hammer. The hurt echoed inside her with little ripples that made her shake. Could she and Tristan have been like Lacy and Mark if she hadn't shoved Tristan out of her life? Tonight was supposed to be a distraction, but seeing this house, like the one in her dream, made her think of him. The way he'd kissed her, the way his body had curled around hers in bed, and how they'd shared some of the most intimate parts of themselves with each other. He hadn't been a future earl with a hundred notches on his bedpost, just a wonderful, sexy man.

And he'd been all mine for one night.

Why had she thought the way she felt about him

was something she could ignore? Sure it had hit fast and hard, like lightning in clear skies, but maybe that was how it was supposed to be? A sudden rush, a fall, and then a jarring landing back on real ground.

"Kat, catch up!" Mark called out.

"I'm coming!" She hadn't realized she'd stopped walking until Mark had shouted at her. There she was, just standing there, lost in thought. As she started walking again, she looked at the house, and it stole her breath.

The house—Fox Hill—with its old cottage manor architecture highlighted by the golden illumination of light from within looked like a home from a fairy tale, a place of magic and dreams, shrouded by a lacy veil of snow.

Mark and Lacy moved more quickly than she did, and when she finally caught up with them at the front of door, a woman was there to meet them. A woman Kat recognized instantly.

Celia. Tristan's stunning cousin.

"Welcome!" Celia beamed.

She wore a black sheath dress and a pair of knee-high black boots that gave her that perfect blend of sexy and classy, a 1960s British Mod look that Kat could never seem to achieve.

Shuffling nervously, Kat tugged her coat closer about her shoulders, feeling self-conscious about her own clothes. Like a child trying to play dress-up compared to Celia's put-together perfection.

"I'm Celia," their hostess said as she ushered them inside.

Fox Hill's interior had red painted walls with dark wood paneling. Evergreen garlands wound around the banister leading upstairs. Music echoed against the walls and ceiling and mixed with the laughter of guests, filling the hall and rooms around them.

Christmas cheer and the end of exams had put everyone in a good mood.

A lively band played covers of popular songs in the large room just to the right. With shelves of endless books, it had to be the library. The spines glinted with gold lettering that winked and shimmered beneath the decorative Christmas lights strung across the wooden ceiling beams. It was cozy and elegant at the same time.

A group of undergrads she vaguely recognized from her dorm walked past, clutching glasses of wine and laughing. Everyone was so relieved exams were over, as she was. But it had been a lot harder to focus on schoolwork when her mind seemed determined to distract her with thoughts of Tristan and how she'd screwed everything up.

"Drinks and other refreshments are in the kitchen straight ahead. Past that, there are plenty of rooms for talking and dancing," Celia explained as she walked them through the lower level of the house.

Kat paused at the foot of stairs, her gaze traveling up the carpeted steps. A strange need to go up them was almost irresistible. She settled one foot on the bottom stair, but Lacy touched her shoulder.

"Kat, Celia's going to show us the house."

Without a word, she followed her friends on the tour, only half-listening to Celia describe the house in between the discussions about professors and holiday plans. After half an hour, she slipped away from the group and headed back to the stairs.

She needed a minute to think and catch her breath. Should she ask Celia about Tristan? Would his cousin give her his cell phone number?

No, that was stupid. She couldn't ask Celia for that. *It's over, whatever shot I had with him, I blew it.*

With a little shake, she forced herself to focus on the party, and the fact that she should be celebrating, having *fun*. But as miserable as she felt right now, it was the last thing she wanted to do. She used to think she was above pity parties and moping, but ever since Tristan had walked out her door, everything in her world seemed...*dimmer*.

Maybe she could distract herself by exploring the house. Lacy had been right about that, getting to snoop around a house like this was the equivalent of catnip to a history major.

It was certainly an old house, at least a century. Kat started up the stairs, slipping her gloves off to stroke her fingers over the smooth, polished wood of the banister. As she climbed, the party sounds grew muted.

At the top of the stairs she glanced down the left and right halls before deciding to go to the right. It was nosy, she had to admit, to want to peek into every room as she walked by but there was no way she would miss out on the chance to do just that. Most were bedrooms, sumptuously decorated in that rich English country-house style she'd seen in movies and decorating magazines. Elegant homes with canopy beds and portraits of people hanging on the walls.

The last door she opened revealed a dark room, but she could see a fire lit in the hearth. And the silhouette of a man sitting in one of the chairs facing the fireplace, holding a glass of either Scotch or brandy. The light trapped in the glass seemed to make the drink burn like liquid fire.

The last thing she wanted was to get caught sneaking around. She retreated a step, hit her elbow on the doorjamb, and cursed. The man in the chair shifted, starting to turn her way.

"Excuse me," she mumbled and took another step backward. Whoever this was probably wanted to be left alone.

"It's fine—" The man leaned around the edge of

the chair then shot to his feet and took a step in her direction. "Kat?" That rich, accented voice made her insides turn to honey. It also halted her dead in her tracks.

"Tristan?" *What was he doing here? Had Celia invited him? She must have, since this was her house.*

He didn't move closer, just stood there, the glass in his hand, watching her. A little bit of light from the hallway illuminated his face. He looked different from the last time she'd seen him. There was a dangerous edge to him, as though he'd gone through hell and come back...darker. What had happened to him?

"Katherine...it's good to see you," he said, as though carefully selecting his words.

Heat rushed to her face, and she was grateful for the dim lighting. Was he still furious with her? She'd understand if he was, but she wanted to talk, to explain...to beg him to give her another chance. It was her fault, this gaping void between them. She hadn't wanted to believe he wasn't seeing Brianna. But he'd called her "Katherine" just now, as though he were reminding himself that he wanted to keep his distance from her.

"What are you doing here?" It was a stupid question, but her mind and mouth apparently weren't communicating.

"I live here." Tristan set his glass down on a small table and took another step forward.

Lord, he moved so beautifully—graceful, sensual, controlled. Her heart raced wildly, and her mouth went dry at the sight of him.

"You live at Fox Hill?" Of course he lived in a fairy-tale house, just like in her dreams.

Was there *anything* about him she could resist? Maybe his sense of entitlement, but it was easy to overlook when everything else about the man was too perfect, too seductive. Kat stood still in the doorway, able to retreat but unwilling. Her heart fluttered, and she tried to control her breathing, but being so close to him filled her with a mix of excitement and nerves.

"It's my mother's. I live here while I'm at university." He took one more step.

Dressed in jeans and a black T-shirt, he looked sexy as hell, his arm flexing as he raised one hand as though to reach for her, before he caught himself and dropped it back to his side.

"I saw your cousin at the door. I thought this was her home."

Tristan shook his head. "She's helping host tonight, but she lives in London."

"Then who was the guy who handed me the invitation?" She thought of the good-looking man with the silver cards.

Tristan chuckled. "Tall as me and blond?"

When she nodded, he chuckled. "That would be Carter. My friend. He lives here at Fox Hill, as well."

"How do you know him?" Kat leaned against the doorjamb. It was wonderful to be talking to him again, after she'd been facing the prospect of never seeing him again. Like sucking in a breath of air after being trapped underwater. The tight ache in her chest that had been suffocating her for the last two weeks seemed to have almost completely vanished.

"Carter's father is the steward of my father's estate. We grew up together. Despite my father's best efforts—" a wry smile twisted his lips "—he couldn't crush our friendship. We've been thick as thieves since we were boys." His tone was so full of affection for Carter that Kat couldn't resist smiling.

It was how she felt about Lacy. Sometimes a person was lucky enough to have a force of nature as a friend, and one couldn't imagine life without them.

Tristan moved closer until he was leaning against the wall next to the door, towering over her. He'd given her plenty of time to escape, but the last thing she wanted was to leave. He'd caught her in his spell. His eyes alone spun black magic around her, and his voice, low and rough, combined with that flirty smile made him irresistible.

"Want to know a secret?" he asked in a silken whisper.

"Yes," she whispered back.

Tristan reached up to cup her cheek, stroking a thumb over her cheekbone. Electric tingles shot from her cheek down to her toes, and she leaned in to the touch. How had she gone so many days without this? She was a fool for thinking she could stop herself from wanting him.

"He's madly in love with Celia, and she with him."

She could picture the two of them, Carter and Celia, a handsome couple, happy and in love. Like a fairy tale. Funny how everything in Tristan's world seemed to make her think of that.

"Are they together?"

He shook his head. "No. Her parents would object. Her mother is my father's younger sister, and unfortunately she's a bit too much like him when it comes to her daughter's relationships."

"But that's—"

"Ridiculous, medieval even. Yet completely normal for our sort." He scowled, his eyes darkening, but she sensed it was out of anger at the truth.

He'd be an earl someday. He'd marry someone important in British society, like Lacy had said. Yet the thought of him with another woman made her stomach turn.

"Kat..." Tristan stared at her, his hungry gaze making her a dizzy. "You should leave."

"Leave?" she echoed, his words stinging like a slap. She had really screwed things up between them.

"Yes." He leaned down the last few inches until

his lips feathered over hers. "Because if you don't leave, I'll lose control. I spent two goddamn weeks without you." The low growl came out of the back of his throat, and it sent shivers down her spine. "Do you know what that's like? Having the thing you want most ripped away from you? I want you, Kat. Bad enough that losing you nearly killed me." He paused, his breath uneven as he stared at her. There was a feral glint in his eyes that sparked her body to life. He wouldn't be gentle, he would be rough, wild, and yet it didn't frighten her even though she knew it should have.

"I'm not leaving," she promised him, her body trembling with her need for him.

"You'd better be damned sure darling, because if you stay, I'll take you to bed and fuck you for the rest of the night. I've spent too much time fantasizing about it. I won't be able to control myself if you stay."

At this suggestion, all rationality fled. She barely knew him. Yet after spending a night in his arms, sharing their secrets, she did know some hidden part of him. A part she didn't want to let go. Kat needed to be with him as much as she needed her next breath. She wasn't going to miss this chance.

She curled her arms around his neck and brushed her lips against his. "Then take me to bed."

Tristan wrapped his arms around her body, one hand coming up to grip the back of her neck, the possessive hold sparking everything inside her to life. His taste, like the brandy he'd been drinking, was thick and rich upon her tongue as he kissed her.

Kissing him was addictive.

Can't get enough. Never enough.

She dug her fingers into his hair, tugging at the strands, urging him to be rougher, to kiss her harder. Everything around them faded away, and she was locked inside her own private universe with Tristan.

He made her feel alive, sexy, like a woman in ways she'd never felt before. As though she was a seductress, a strong, beautiful woman who could have this handsome man in her bed. That silly feeling of being a naive college girl who didn't know anything about love or life melted away beneath his kiss. Tristan had introduced her to both in a few short weeks. Even when he'd been out of her life, she hadn't been able to escape thoughts of him. She hadn't wanted to, either.

Take me, she begged him with her kiss.

With a low animalistic sound, he gripped her by the waist and lifted her up against his body. Carrying her over to a desk in the study, he cleared the surface of its contents with a swipe of his hand. The items hit the floor with a crash, the papers fluttering.

He set her down and continued to kiss her ruthlessly. He was conquering every part of her body and soul with every wicked slant of his mouth, and she loved it. She tugged at his shirt, trying to lift it, needing to get closer.

"Darling, I want you...but we need an *actual* bed," he moaned against her mouth.

His exploring hands and near-frantic kisses heightened the throb of desire between her legs. She was a live wire, and one touch in the right spot and would set her off. Her hands scrambled over his clothes, trying to find a way to get to his skin, remembering all too well how he looked in nothing but boxers.

"No bed," she clawed at him. "Here, now—"

"Maybe I need to take the edge off you."

His husky words were Kat's only warning before he jerked her legs apart. He held onto the back of her neck with one hand, while his other slid up her inner thigh, pushing her dress up to her hips. Then he cupped her mound, the heat of his palm against her throbbing clit making her jerk and gasp.

"You like that?" Tristan rubbed her clit through her panties, swirling a fingertip over the nub. It was almost *too* sensitive.

Kat's hands slipped beneath his shirt. She raked her nails down his back at the same moment he dipped a finger past her panties and stroked her opening.

God, his voice, he could say anything with that accent—like a dirty-talking Knight of the Round Table or something—and she'd explode. A desperate moan escaped her. How had she gone straight to Arthurian erotic fantasies with him?

"I need the words, darling. Be that naughty little kitty Kat for me."

Another wonderful, wicked stroke of his thumb, a feather of his lips on her jaw, and a slight squeeze on her neck, all reminded her how helpless she was to resist anything he wanted to do to her. He was a true British bad boy, and it was turning on everything inside her.

"Tristan, *please*," she panted, her hips canting in the direction of his finger.

"Please what? Say it for me, Kat," he ordered. His hand at the nape of her neck fisted in her hair, jerking slightly on the strands, giving her a hint of pain, which only made her skin flush with an unbearable heat.

She was too shy to demand he fuck her with his fingers, too embarrassed to be so bold. But she wanted to be able to tell him exactly what he should do to her to make her come, not that he needed any hints. It was like the man could read her mind. In silent begging, she shifted her body closer and finally pleaded with him, "Touch me, *harder*."

With a gentle nip at her lips, he did exactly what she wanted and thrust one finger into her. The world seemed to blossom with new colors, and everything started to spin.

"Oh, God!" she hissed and writhed against his hand, so close to coming.

He nuzzled her neck, leaving hot, teasing kisses as he caged her body against his with one arm while his other hand began to slowly fuck her. Each slow, deliberate penetration of that one finger was devastating and perfect, like the night in her dorm room only a thousand times stronger.

"There's so much I want to do to you, little kitty Kat," he purred in that soft, velvety accent.

It was all she needed. A sudden explosion of pleasure overtook her, and she spasmed around his finger. Her teeth sank into his shirt-clad shoulder as she rode the intense orgasm.

"Bloody hell," he muttered, panting against her

ear. "You're destroying my self-control." He chuckled, before he nibbled her neck. "You're going to unman me, at this rate."

She laughed. Unman the sexiest guy she'd ever met? *Unlikely.*

He kissed her again, taking his time with leisurely licks and nips. His finger was still inside her, drawing out the trembling aftershocks of pleasure. Her muscles clamped down on him again and again, trying to keep him there.

A wave of shyness hit her, and she buried her face against his chest, her hands still stroking the hot muscles beneath his black shirt. Reality crept back bit by bit as the high of her orgasm faded, and she realized she was sitting on the edge of an antique desk in a fire-lit library with Tristan standing between her thighs. It was wanton, sexy, and Kat couldn't help but feel strange because she'd never dreamed she'd be *this* kind of woman.

She was the girl who stayed at home and did her homework, went to bed early, got to class and just... worked. But here she was with Tristan, and he was opening up a new, darker side to her, one that felt older, more aware of the world and of what a man and woman could be together. A shiver rippled through her.

"Are you all right?" he asked, and buried his face against the crown of her hair.

"Yes." She smiled up at him and wriggled to get closer. "You're so hot."

"Need me to warm you up?" he asked, his low, rumbling laugh creating a new ripple of excitement and contentment inside her.

"Hmm, that would be nice." She pressed her cheek against his throat, breathing in his clean, dark scent. It was addictive. She wanted to bottle up that scent and take it everywhere.

When he withdrew his hand from between her thighs, she hated the emptiness.

With a little wicked grin, Tristan raised his finger to his lips, sucking it, his eyes briefly closing as he tasted...her. God, he was licking his finger, the one that had been inside her.

"I always knew you'd taste sweet." He opened his eyes and stared at her with a hungry intensity that made her entire body ripple with another mini-orgasm.

He pulled her dress down her legs, and she slid off the desk. For a second she worried that the night was over, but when she looked up at his face and saw the fire in his gaze and the wicked tilt of his lips in a sinful smile, she knew things were far from over.

"What do you say we try a bed this time?"

Tristan held out a hand, and she tucked her fingers into his. He gave a little tug, and she followed him out of the study. Music and laughter echoed up from the hallway near the stairs, but Kat could barely hear it above the wild pounding of her heart. They walked down the hallway, and he stopped at a room, opening the door. The dark interior was inviting rather than frightening.

"Your bedroom?" she asked.

She could barely believe that this was going to happen. She was going to have sex with Tristan in his room. Her first time...with him, with any man. But with him, it meant everything.

"Yes." He grasped the little brass key sticking out of the door and, with a slow turn, locked her inside with him. Another skitter of her pulse, and she had to swallow to keep calm. How could he make her feel a little scared and so wildly excited at the same time?

She stood there taking in the room while he disappeared into the connecting bathroom and ran water in the sink as he washed his hands.

The large four-poster bed was made of rich dark wood, the posts carved with leaves and swirling vines. Kat bent and unzipped her ankle boots, sliding them off. She stood by the foot of the bed and wriggled her toes in the thick cream carpet.

Everything in the room was rich and decadent, but also understated. From the navy blue silk coverlet and the thick pillows piled invitingly on the bed, to the black and white photographs of parts of Cambridge which hung on the walls? Tristan had quite a room.

"What do you think?" Tristan came up behind her, his hands settling on her hips.

Kat turned her head and rubbed it against him. It was so hard to think straight when he was touching her, and even harder knowing they were going to...

"It's a lot better than my dorm room..."

Bigger bed. Softer sheets. I can do this. I want to do this.

He pressed his cheek against the crown of her hair before his hands tugged at the zipper of her dress.

"I missed you," he whispered. The way he said it, with a mixture of confession and epiphany, made it seem as though he was surprised to admit it.

"I missed you, too," she admitted. "I'm sorry about what I said." She held her breath.

His hands froze in the middle of pulling down her dress.

"Why?"

Kat reached up to shimmy her dress down her shoulders. It dropped to the floor, and she stepped out of it. Would talking about this make things worse? It would probably kill the moment, but she owed him an apology.

"I'm sorry for judging you. I should've given you a fair chance." Kat rotated in his arms, aware she was wearing nothing but a black bra and panties. She hoped—no, she prayed—he'd still want her.

His eyes raked down her body, and she clenched her thighs together at the hot hunger she saw in his gaze.

"Consider it forgiven. Before I met you...I was that kind of man. But no longer. Not while I'm with *you*." Tristan cupped her face, and their gazes locked. Then he began to press teasing, soft kisses on her, his hands stroking her hair, making her shiver even as he tamed her frantically beating heart.

She held her breath and then nodded. "Please don't hurt me. If we do this, I want you to promise me that." She meant emotionally, he had to know that. She wasn't afraid he'd hurt her physically.

Tristan gripped the back of her neck, holding her still so she couldn't shy away during the most vulnerable moment of her life.

"I can't erase my past, and sometimes it resurfaces. If you can trust me, nothing will hurt you while we're together." His promise was a husky whisper, but his eyes were sharp with sincerity.

Kat tried not to think about his past, his playboy reputation, and the scores of women he'd been with before. It was a little easier, at least right now, to push it all aside because she *wanted* to trust him.

"Okay." With a smile, she gripped the bottom of his T-shirt and tugged it up. He helped her lift the fabric off, and he tossed it away. But when she reached for his jeans, he caught her hands.

"Leave them. If we don't, I'll be inside you too soon, and I want to fuck you all night, darling. Don't test me until I've regained some control."

His words made her shiver. She'd never cared all that much for the word *fuck* but when Tristan said it to her...it made her skin burn and clit pulse in time with her wild heartbeat.

Tristan lifted her up by her waist and carried her the short distance to the bed. He tossed her onto her back, but before she could react, he'd crawled up her body, only pausing to unfasten the button of his jeans. But he didn't remove them. The promise of unbuttoned denim was somehow hotter. God, what this man did to her.

When he noticed her watching him, he grinned. "The last thing I need is one bloody button stopping me once I'm ready to be inside you."

Her face flamed, and she ducked her head. He placed a kiss over her brow and nudged her knees apart with one of his.

"Can we get beneath the covers?" Kat asked. This was her first time a man was seeing her naked, and she wanted to hide as much as possible.

Tristan was watching her with a concerned expression in his eyes. "Are you cold?"

When she shook her head, he raised a brow. "Then, no. I want to see you, Kat. Every inch of you. Covers are for later, *much* later. When it's time to sleep."

"But—"

He kissed away all of her protests. She clung to his broad shoulders, encouraging him to put more of his weight on top of her. It was a good feeling, his hot, hard body over hers, pressing her down into the soft bed. Tiny shivers of excitement rippled through her.

"Maybe I should warm you up," he teased.

She couldn't help but beam at him. She was so nervous that it felt like every muscle inside her was shaking, but she wanted him, and that desire battled against her nerves.

"Tristan, I haven't done a whole lot," she whispered.

"I know, darling."

How could he soothe and entice her at the same time with so simple a reassurance?

"I haven't done *this* at all, remember?" She closed her eyes, then opened them again, ready to face him and however he might react.

He touched her cheek. "Kat, we don't have to do this if you're not ready."

She let out a soft husky laugh. "I want this and I'm ready, I'm just nervous. What if I'm not good at it? You've been with so many other girls who were probably great in bed..." What if she didn't measure up? The idea was enough to start cooling her fires.

The flames of desire in his eyes simmered to a softer, low-burning heat. "You're not simply a notch in my bedpost. Do you understand? We do this if and when you're ready."

Her heart fluttered, and she was too afraid to hope. "Do you mean that?"

With a little smile, he laughed. "Yes, I do. I can't figure out why, but you're important to me, Kat. So if you aren't ready for this, we can take it slow, even if it bloody well kills me." His chuckle was rough, as though he were clinging to the last shreds of his control.

God, how she loved knowing she put him on the edge like that.

"And if I do want to do this?" She slid closer to him on the bed.

Tristan grinned. "Then we do it, however you want."

Kat leaned forward and kissed him. "Let's do this."

"You trust me?" he asked her.

"I do." She ran her fingertips along his clean-shaven jaw, admiring how soft his skin was, and knowing it would tickle her in a few hours when a beard started to shadow his jaw again.

"Then touch me, mark me, do anything you want. I'll make this a night to remember," he promised.

After that, words weren't needed. He tugged the cups of her bra down, revealing her breasts. He licked, then sucked at each nipple, teasing the tips until they were so sensitive even his warm exhalations against them drew a whimper from her.

Kat had never known her instincts could be so strong, but they took over.

She arched up, thrusting her breasts deeper into his waiting mouth. Her hands roamed his back, shaping the smooth, hard contours of his shoulder blades, the indentation of his spine. Closing her eyes, she embraced every sensation from the muted music of the party below, the slide of her skin on the sheets, and the way her body fit Tristan's.

One of his hands cupped her ass. With a little sting against her skin, he ripped her panties off and tossed them aside, growling against her breasts as he did so. There was an animal side to him, one that excited and fascinated her. The cool, seductive British sex god turned into a raw sensual beast. The realization only made her wetter.

She tried to clamp her thighs together. He answered with a low groan of approval and bit one of her nipples. Her nails sank into his back, dragging down his shoulder blades as an orgasm started to build inside her. Kat raised her hips, rubbing her clit against the hard ridge behind his jeans.

Kat bit her bottom lip, holding in all the sounds that she wanted to make. Somewhere in the back of her mind, she was all too aware that her friends and his were downstairs partying. The last thing either of them wanted was to be overheard by anyone who might venture down the hall. She rocked her body up, desperate to get closer.

He reached down between their bodies and unzipped his jeans. His erect length bumped her thighs as he shifted and then lifted her hips. She almost laughed at the intimacy of this moment, him fumbling, losing that cool exterior, his breath panting as hard as hers.

"Hold that thought, darling," he whispered, shifting off her slightly to reach over to a nightstand. He yanked open the top drawer a few inches, his hands rifling through the contents of the drawer until he pulled out a silver square. He tore the packet open with his teeth and hastily slid the condom over his erect cock.

Kat ducked her head a few inches, and her cheeks flamed with heat. She wanted to watch him put it on, but she was too shy to let him know she was watching.

"You ready for me?" He feathered his lips over hers.

Kat answered with a shaky nod.

"Tell me if I get too rough." Tristan's murmur against her neck had her shivering in new excitement.

"Fuck," he groaned, then positioned himself between her thighs. "Tell me you can take it hard." He was almost begging, his word ragged and rough.

"Yeah." The word was barely out of her mouth before he thrust in.

Hard. Pain seared her inside, but she breathed through it. She was so turned on, that even the pain of her virginity being taken didn't last long, not when Tristan kissed her with that raw, open-mouthed hunger that seduced her completely, reducing her to a pure primal woman.

The sudden tightness, the almost suffocating fullness overwhelmed her. For a second she couldn't breathe. She felt...*owned*.

He waited, seemingly content to kiss her while

their bodies remained joined, but his muscles were tense beneath her exploring palms.

When their mouths broke apart, he whispered, "How do you feel? Is there a lot of pain?"

With a shiver, she shook her head. "Not much, I'm okay, I think. Don't stop kissing me." Her thighs clenched tight around his hips, and she rocked against him in encouragement.

Tristan braced his body above hers, his arm muscles flexing on either side of her head as he stole her mouth with his again. His tongue entered in slow, deliberate thrusting motions, echoing the movement of his hips. But the jerk of his pelvis increased in speed. Sharp, deep penetrations, hitting a sweet spot over and over again.

Brilliant stars burst in front of her eyes.

"Like that?" he growled in her ear.

She could only answer with a soft whimper of pleasure.

He drove into her again and again. The headboard slammed against the wall—*bam-bam-bam*.

"So good, so fucking good, Kat."

Their mouths broke apart, and he continued that almost violent pounding, but his words, whispered harshly, were rushed, as though he could barely think. It would have made her smile if she could find any strength left to control her face. Her world shattered in tingles, then hard explosions, and silent cries of ecstasy, the likes of which she'd never experienced.

"Kat, darling," he moaned, his body shaking hard above hers, his muscles quivering as much as hers as he came, too.

Now she understood when Lacy joked about how some nights she couldn't walk after she and Mark had sex. Kat was positive if she tried to move off the bed, she'd fall flat on her face.

"Kat," Tristan whispered as he leaned in to kiss

her. The wild, animal look that had been in his eyes had vanished. In its place was a feral protectiveness that was softened by affection. That startled her, but she couldn't deny the skittering response in her heart.

"Tristan." She laughed breathlessly and lifted a hand to brush his dark hair back so she could see his eyes. God, she adored his eyes.

His body tensed and his hips gave a small jerk in natural response to her touch. He wasn't hard like before, but he still filled her and the sudden push against her swollen tissues made her suck in a breath.

"Sorry, darling," he apologized, with another leisurely kiss. "How do you feel now?"

"Like I'll never walk again," she said, completely honest.

Tristan's smile faded.

"In a good way. That was the best I've ever had," Kat hastily added.

He trailed a finger down her cheek. "Considering you've never been with a man before, I'm not sure that's a compliment."

"It is. I've never felt like this with *anyone*..."

Confessing that, telling him, even in the darkness of his room and in the warm embrace of his arms, made her afraid he'd laugh at her, tell her that she was a fool for feeling that way.

He beamed. "I was only teasing."

The truly happy expression on his face was such a delight that she grinned back. He was so unguarded, unjaded with her at that moment. Perhaps it wouldn't last, but she'd enjoy this as long as she could.

"I like it when you tease me." She brushed the back of her knuckles over his cheek and he leaned in to the caress. It made her body quiver with a secret joy.

It's just the two of us, but it feels like the entire world is in this room with us, ours of the taking, for the living. An adventure at last.

The cool air made her skin break out into goose bumps.

"Now can we get under the covers?" She circled one of his nipples with her index finger. His focus dropped to his chest, watching her finger tease him.

"We can now." Tristan caught her hand and raised it to his lips, kissing her palm.

They pulled the covers back. Kat was so limp and exhausted she flopped ungracefully between the sheets. Tristan swatted her bottom, and she squealed, rolling over to stare at him.

"What was that for?" she demanded, but the wicked glint in his eyes made her want to giggle.

He wiggled his brows. "Some bottoms are made for spanking."

Before she could stop him, he smacked her ass again, creating a bare hint of a sting that warmed instead of hurt.

"You have a kinky side, don't you?" Kat remembered his leather belt. With another guy, it might've scared her, but not him. He'd proven he was worthy of her trust. And she trusted herself around him enough to admit that she'd like to explore that edgier side to sex with him someday.

"A little," Tristan agreed, pulling the covers up over her. He left the bed and went into the bathroom to dispose of the condom. She heard water running a minute before he came back to the bed. He settled in beside her and tugged her back against his body.

It struck Kat in that moment. She'd had sex with Tristan. She wasn't a virgin anymore.

They were naked, cuddled up in his bed. It was insane, but oh so wonderful. She was with Tristan, just them in his bed, bodies pressed together, limbs entwined. Sweet and tender after the intensity of what they'd just shared.

"Stay the night," he whispered, shifting closer. "Tell your friends you're staying. I can take you back to the dorm in the morning."

The man was the devil, offering up a sweet temptation she couldn't resist.

"Okay." She looked up at him. "Can you get my coat? I left it in the study. My phone's in the pocket. I'll call Lacy and let her know."

"Done." He kissed her before sliding out of bed and pulling his jeans on. He paused at the door to look back at her. The sight of him in nothing but unbuttoned jeans flushed her body with a new wave of heat. The tender spot between her thighs throbbed and she clenched her legs together.

"I'm glad you came tonight." He dropped his gaze, but it was too dark to see if her British playboy was blushing.

Surely not. He could be with *anyone*. Having her here had to be only a temporary satisfaction. He'd move on, but for now he was hers, and she wanted to enjoy every minute she had with him.

The idea was bitter to swallow, but she managed to resurrect her smile.

"Me, too."

He nodded, patted the door frame, and then disappeared.

Kat's smile faded, and she slid back down in Tristan's bed, feeling very small and alone. She'd made the choice to be with him. The question was, how long would it last? And would she be able to keep her heart safe?

❦ 16 ❦

When Tristan returned to his bedroom, Kat was already asleep, snuggled in his blankets, using one pillow as if she was clutching a stuffed animal. The sight created an odd blend of warmth and hunger inside him.

He didn't have the heart to wake her, so he dug through the coat's pockets until he found her phone. He scrolled through the contacts until he saw *Lacy* listed. Standing just outside his bedroom, he listened to the phone. On the third ring, Lacy answered.

"Kat, where are you? Mark and I are freaking out."

"Lacy, this is Tristan Kingsley. Kat has asked me to inform you she's spending the night here with me. I'll bring her back to the dorm tomorrow morning."

In the background he heard laughter and music, which meant Lacy and Mark were still downstairs somewhere.

"Put her on the phone," Lacy ordered.

"She's asleep. I won't wake her."

"I don't care if you happen to be the most eligible bachelor in London. Put her on the bloody phone or so help me, I'll search every room in this house until

I find you, and you won't like what I'll do when I get my hands on you."

Her fierce protectiveness earned his respect.

"Very well, but I don't like having to wake her when she needs rest." He also didn't want her to reconsider staying the night with him. If Lacy talked her out of it, Kat might grab her clothes and run from him again. More than anything, he wanted her to stay right there in his bed...with him.

He didn't miss the snarl on the other end of the phone.

"Did you sleep with her?" Lacy demanded.

Tristan ignored her as he sat on the edge of the bed and shook Kat's shoulder.

"Kat, Lacy wants to speak with you." He handed Kat the cell phone as she sat up. Blinking, she brushed the waves of her hair out of her face. Seeing her all mussed and rumpled stirred Tristan's body to life all over again.

She took the phone, yawned, and put it to her ear. "Lacy?"

Even from two feet away, Tristan could hear Lacy's tirade in a high-pitched screech. Kat sighed and held the phone about six inches away while she listened to Lacy's admonition.

"I'm staying here tonight," she said, wrinkling her nose. When more screeching occurred she spoke again. "I'm fine, I'll explain everything later, okay?"

The yelling tapered off, and Kat's gaze flicked to Tristan. Her lips curved in a shy smile.

"Yeah...I promise, I'll talk to you tomorrow." She disconnected and tossed her mobile off to the far side of the bed.

He raised an eyebrow. "Everything all right with your friend?"

She tugged the covers up as she seemed to realize

that her breasts were exposed. "Oh, yeah. She's just protective of me, that's all."

"I'm glad you have friends like that," he said.

He stood and unzipped his jeans. The responding blush on her face as she watched him strip out of them was rewarding. He loved how she responded to him and the way she seemed caught off guard by her innate sensuality.

Her lips were slightly parted, her hair a wonderful tumble of color, like Sleeping Beauty brought to life in a faraway tower with a kiss. The fantasies she created in his mind were sensual and powerful. Everything about Kat was unusual and fascinated him.

Passion awakened for his Katherine, *his* Kat.

"Have you ever slept naked before?" he asked as he climbed back into bed.

She shook her head. Another deep blush spread from her face to the tips of her breasts.

"You're tempting me, darling." Tristan leaned over and teased her lips with his before he gave in to kissing her fully. After a minute, he pulled away. "Now go to sleep." He laughed at her put-out expression.

She rolled to face him, one arm stretched out. Kat paused, as though catching herself. Her eyelashes fanned up and down as she fell asleep again.

Tristan reached for her, curling an arm around her waist. She reacted by cuddling against him, holding on to him like she had the pillow.

In the past, he hadn't been too fond of his lovers staying the night. There was too much intimacy when people slept together, sharing breaths, their dreams close enough to collide. But with Kat, he wanted to hold her, feel her heartbeat, and listen to her breathe.

It was clear she craved the same physical connection he did.

"Thank you," she murmured. Her words were muffled by her drowsiness, her eyes still closed.

"For what?" he asked, trying not to laugh at her stubborn fight against sleep.

"Tonight. I found out recently that my dad—" she paused— "is dating someone. It's been...hard for me the last week, trying to adjust and everything." She rubbed her cheek against his shoulder, and the action filled his chest with a cottony warmth.

There she was, opening up to him about what she was thinking and feeling. It was everything he thought he didn't want when it came to women and relationships, but with Kat, he *wanted* to know her inside and out.

"I'm sorry." He tightened his grip around her. "I know how you feel. My mother has also started dating, too. I'm not thrilled. The last man she dated was an absolute cad. I'll have to inspect this man before he receives my approval." It felt good to know he wasn't the only one having to accept his parent dating again. His mother was a beautiful woman, and it shouldn't have shocked him as much as it did that she was seeing a man romantically.

"'Approval'? You sound like royalty." Kat giggled, the sleepy sound going straight to his cock. He wanted to roll over on top of her and give her something to laugh about. But they'd already done enough for her first time. She'd be sore.

He stroked her waist as they talked, amused that this was...pleasant. Talking with a woman had never been enjoyable before, not after sex, at any rate. He'd always felt trapped when he couldn't get a woman to leave his bed fast enough. Now he wanted to find ways to make Kat stay.

"Why do I sense that my acting 'like royalty' isn't a compliment?"

Kat shrugged a shoulder. "Whatever you say, *my lord.*"

He stroked her body beneath the covers, enjoying

the feel of her, pressed skin-to-skin with him. "I'll be an earl one day. It's not royalty, but it is the peerage."

"The peerage," she echoed in a British accent and giggled again. The sound was infectious, and it made him laugh, too.

"What's so funny?"

Kat, eyes still closed, hugged him a little tighter. "I'll tell you in the morning." She was so close to sleep, he didn't have the heart to keep her awake.

"All right, darling. Sweet dreams." He kissed her brow and held her as she drifted to sleep.

Tristan wasn't tired, and for some reason, he was perfectly content to hold Kat and count the faint freckles on her shoulders. He wanted to memorize the sight of her pert little nose and her long dark lashes. He didn't wish to be anywhere else or with anyone else.

What the bloody hell is happening to me?

K at sat in the back of the cab, clutching her duffle bag, backpack, and cell phone. As the driver pulled onto a side street in London's West End, she checked her messages. Tristan had been texting her most of the morning.

Miss you, kitty Kat. Wish you were with me now so I could make you purr.

With a little grin she tapped back.

I miss you too, especially your bed.

It would've been hard to be so teasing and intimate with someone else, but it was easy with Tristan, especially after everything they'd shared and done. He made it so easy to have fun and act a little reckless.

His response was immediate.

Fuck, darling. I'm trying to be on my best behavior and you're making it hard. I have to meet my mother's boyfriend. He'll be here soon. Seems like we're both meeting our new families today. I'll text you when I have a chance.

Grinning happily, she waited a few minutes as the driver made a U-turn to pull up before a row of town houses.

The driver glanced at her through the rearview mirror.

"This is it, miss."

She handed him a few pound notes to cover the cab fare and stepped out onto the pavement in front of a large, expensive-looking town house. The frosted windows glittered with Christmas lights and tinsel. The pavement leading to the front door was meticulously cleared of snow.

Her father was somewhere inside this house with his new girlfriend. For a brief moment, new strength surged into her. After spending a wonderful night with Tristan only a day ago, she felt strangely...brave. As though she could conquer the world. Including meeting the woman who had won her father's heart.

Gripping her coat tightly, she shivered from the cold. Memories of Tristan's kisses, his sweet, whispered words from the night before, warmed her anew. She would carry those memories with her like a shield into battle. It wasn't easy thinking of the possibility of a stepmother, but knowing Tristan wanted her, cared about her, made her feel a little less alone and able to face what was to come. And soon, she would see him again, perhaps while he, too, was in London for the holidays.

Her phone buzzed again and she swung her bag over her shoulder, tugged one of her gray mittens off with her teeth, and tapped the screen. It was a text from Tristan.

Kat...we have to talk.

His words made a responding flutter of nerves in her belly.

What's the matter?

But he didn't respond to the text. Kat stared at the phone for a second longer. She couldn't delay meeting her dad and his girlfriend. Whatever Tristan had to tell her would have to wait, even if the thought of what he might say would be bad. No one ever started out a good conversation with "We have to talk." But she couldn't worry about that, not until she got through this meet-and-greet with her dad.

God, this was going to be so awkward.

"Katherine!" Her father met her at the sidewalk leading up to the town house and swung her duffle bag over his shoulder.

It took a moment to adjust to the sight of her father. The man she'd left on the bus station platform when she'd gone to Cambridge four months ago had been stiff, in a suit, his face lined with stress and fatigue. The man who embraced her now was in jeans and a sweater, smiling like an idiot. He looked almost a decade younger. The fine lines about his eyes and mouth had almost faded, and he was striding with such energy toward her that she almost didn't believe it was him.

"Honey, I've got big news. I wanted to tell you myself before you meet Lizzy."

Her stomach clenched. "Tell me what?"

Her father's grip on her shoulders tightened a little, and his smile faded as he grew serious.

"I know this feels sudden, but I've given it a lot of thought, and so has Lizzy. I've asked her to marry me, and she's said yes." Her father waited, expecting a response, but all Kat could manage was to sputter one word.

"What?" They both knew she'd heard him, but it was too much too soon. "You're engaged?"

"I know it's a lot to take in, but you'll like her. And her son. You'll have a new stepbrother. Won't that be fun? You've always wanted a sibling."

Stepbrother? Was he kidding? She didn't want a stepbrother. She didn't want a stepmother. She just wanted things to go back to the way they were.

Something in her eyes must have warned him that she was on the verge of breaking apart into a thousand pieces because he said, "I know this is upsetting, honey. I meant to ask her to marry me after I talked to you first, but last night we were alone and having dinner and I just..." He shrugged. "It felt right." Her dad pulled her into a hug. "Please, honey. I know this is a lot to process. Just put on a smile for me and after I introduce you, I'll show you to the guest room Lizzy picked out for you, okay?" He drew back to look at her.

She wanted to run and hide, and there was no doubt he knew it because he was her father and they'd always been close. Just the way she knew that he was truly happy with this woman and that he deserved to be loved.

With a little jerk of a nod, she forced a smile. "I'm happy for you, Dad. Really."

A butler met them at the front door and took Kat's duffle from her father's arms.

"Ms. Roberts? Your other bag?" The man pointed at her backpack.

"Kat, this is Mr. Jeremy. The butler."

"Hello." Kat greeted the middle-aged man who gave her a polite but distant smile.

Lizzy has an honest-to-God butler? How rich is this woman?

Mr. Jeremy nodded. "A pleasure to meet you, Miss Roberts."

"Please call me 'Kat' or 'Katherine,'" she said. The look of horror on his face almost made her laugh.

"Let the poor man alone," her father teased, and handed the backpack over to Mr. Jeremy.

"It was nice to meet you." Kat watched the servant toddle off with her bags. She and her father had had a cook when they lived in Chicago and a housekeeper who cleaned during the day. But Kat wasn't used to having live-in staff like butlers.

"Come on. Lizzy and her son are just in here. I haven't met him yet. I wanted to wait for you to get here." Her father stopped in front of a mahogany door with a lovely gilded handle. It creaked in protest before the door opened.

"Lizzy, sweetheart, Kat's here." Her father put an arm around her shoulder as they entered the room.

It was a drawing room, with warm blue walls painted with yellow flowers, beneath white crown molding trimming the ceiling. A marble fireplace directly opposite the door was bright with a roaring fire.

A man stood with his back to her, one hand braced on the mantel. He had to be Lizzy's son. Something about the way he stood, his dark hair was...familiar. When she tried to get a closer look, a tall, blonde woman who'd been standing close by the door suddenly moved to block Kat's sight of him.

"It's so nice to finally meet you! You're father has told me so much about you. Is it all right if I call you 'Kat'?" Lizzy's beaming smile was infectious.

"Yeah, 'Kat's fine. It's nice to meet you." She froze for a second when Lizzy hugged her, then relaxed at how nice it felt. She was in awe of the woman's natural beauty and warmth. No wonder her father was taken with her.

"Please call me 'Lizzy,'" she said. "And I'd like you to meet my son." She stepped aside and pointed to where the man stood, still facing the fire. Again that eerie sense that she *knew* him, that he was familiar to her...but how could that be? She'd never met Lizzy or her son.

"Tristan, come here and meet your future stepsister."

Tristan?

The name stopped all brain communication to Kat's body. She froze.

The man by the fire, the one in black trousers and

a gray sweater, turned to gaze at her with fathomless blue-green eyes.

The world suddenly tilted and spun around her and she couldn't breathe. Black spots dotted her vision until she sucked in a lungful of air.

The man she thought she'd recognized from behind was Tristan. *Her* Tristan.

This couldn't be happening to her. Life was too cruel to give her something as wonderful as him and steal it away.

Tristan Kingsley, the sexiest, naughtiest man she'd ever known, the man she'd just shared mind-blowing sex with, was going to be her stepbrother?

Holy shit.

THANK YOU SO MUCH FOR READING *FORBIDDEN*!
Keep reading below to start the first 3 chapters of Kat and Tristan's story as it continues in the book *Seduction*!

The best way to know when a new book is released is to do one or all of the following:

Join my Newsletter: http://laurensmithbooks. com/free-books-and-newsletter/

Follow Me on BookBub: https://www.bookbub. com/authors/lauren-smith

Join my Facebook VIP Reader Group called Lauren Smith's League: https://www.facebook. com/groups/400377546765661/

Turn the page to read the first 3 chapters of *Seduction: Love in London Book 2*! Come on, you know you want to turn that page...

SEDUCTION

CHAPTER 1

B*loody Hell.*

Tristan Kingsley was in a dark spiral. Anger and confusion raged beneath his skin like wildfire. His mother had sent his carefully constructed plan toppling down like a house of cards when she'd announced her engagement to an American investment banker.

Her engagement wasn't the *worst* part of the whole situation. No, the fucking demons in hell were laughing at him for the ironic twist his destiny had just taken. Because five minutes ago, Katherine Roberts had walked through the door with her father, Clayton.

My Kat. The girl he'd ruthlessly pursued and sweetly seduced until she'd succumbed and let him take her to bed. The girl he'd fucked so hard she'd had trouble walking the next morning. The girl he'd opened up to about things he'd never shared with anyone. And he still hadn't had enough of her to satisfy his obsession.

My stepsister. Future stepsister. And, two nights ago, they'd rammed his headboard into the wall so hard, it had left gouges in the wallpaper. He'd had rough, wild sex before, but with her... She'd been so innocent, a bloody virgin, but she'd responded like a sex goddess...

I can't think about her anymore. How her body felt underneath me—skin to skin. How perfect she tasted. How she screamed out my name when I exploded inside of her...

Kat hadn't moved from the doorway to the library of his mother's townhouse. The moment she'd come in the door and recognized him she'd frozen. Her face pale, her lips pursed, and her gray eyes wide as saucers. She hadn't known this was coming, just as he hadn't.

It was a bloody nightmare.

They'd left Cambridge separately for their Christmas holidays, each facing the same situation. His mother had told him that she was in a relationship with someone, and Kat's father had told her the same. Neither he nor Kat could have guessed that their parents had met in London and started dating. Or gotten engaged. It was a strange, and now damnable, coincidence. Of all the eligible men in London his mother could have met and fallen in love with, it had to be Kat's father?

At twenty-five years old and working toward his Master's in business, Tristan could afford little time for distractions, aside from the string of nameless girls he'd slept with before Kat. He had classes and the pressures of his father's estate looming over him. That was the price he had to pay for being the future Earl of Pembroke.

Until he'd walked into the Pickerel Inn pub one night and his world had changed forever. Kat, a luscious, intoxicating first-year undergraduate, had walked up to the bar for a drink and they'd talked. Something had seemed to pull them together, like invisible strings. She'd leaned up on her tiptoes and kissed him. The way she'd felt in his arms, her lips melding with his... In an instant he'd gone from a man who could have any woman he wanted to a man who wanted *only* her. She was nineteen, and so inexperienced, he wanted to drag her back to his bed and never let her leave until he'd shown her everything he knew about the art of sexual pleasure.

My obsession, my erotic fantasy. Mine. All mine.

At least she had been until his mum had blown his plans to hell with the news that Kat was going to be his stepsister. As a stepsister, a family relation, she'd be untouchable. Their parents simply wouldn't allow it. He'd had plenty of encounters with protective fathers in the past when stories of women he'd seduced had come out in the papers. But Tristan had always held his ground, had never done the honorable thing and married any of those girls. It was just sex. This wasn't the Victorian era. If a woman went to bed with him, that was her choice and no father could demand Tristan that do anything afterward.

I've never been a saint. I certainly can't be one now, not when I want Kat as badly as I do. But how was he going to get Kat all to himself if his mother and her father were watching over them both during the holidays? He'd have to find a way to keep their relationship a secret. It was the only solution. And if the paparazzi ever got wind of his affair with Kat, his father would have him executed in the square of the London Tower just to make a point.

Kat was completely unsuitable—at least she would be in his father's eyes. And for the moment, his father still had a firm grip on Tristan's future, including whom he could date. As an American with no titles, no connections, and no vast fortune, she offered nothing that his father would approve of. Tristan clenched his jaw. He despised that his father had so much control over his life, but that was how it had always been. As the only heir to the estate, he had a duty to the land and the people who worked on it to keep things afloat. His father still controlled the family purse strings, and Tristan knew he couldn't abandon the estate.

Knowing his father would never approve of Kat didn't stop Tristan from wanting her, and it certainly didn't deter him from his intent to sleep with her again. It simply made him all the more aware that he'd have to be careful about how he got her back into his bed so that no parents could discover them.

His mother, Elizabeth, was still standing by Kat, and she made a tiny gesture with her head, encouraging him to come over to his future stepsister. All he wanted to do was walk over and kiss Kat senseless... but their parents were staring at him.

I ought to get out of here before I make an arse of myself.

How was he going to survive three weeks with Kat under the same roof and not touch her whenever he wanted?

"Tristan, don't be rude. Stop sulking by the fireplace, come over here and say hello," his mother hissed in admonishment.

He walked over to Kat and held out a hand, pretending they'd never met, never touched, *never* shared his bed, exploring each other's bodies. It was harder than he expected to resist reacting to her. He smiled politely, fighting off the urge to chuckle when her pale cheeks blossomed with color.

She must be remembering, as he was, how it had felt when he'd pinned her down and made her beg for him to do a thousand dirty, erotic things to her. And he had, oh, he had. And that was making it so hard to keep from reacting with the intimacy he desired. There wouldn't be a scorching kiss, no stroking of hands. Not while their parents watched them with hawk-like precision.

"It's lovely to meet you, Kat." He sucked in a breath as she slowly took his hand and shook it.

Sparks of heat burst between their palms, that undeniable chemistry that drew him like a planet orbiting a star. Cosmic, inescapable. This was why he couldn't walk away, why he had to touch her, keep her close to him. She was the first woman that had fascinated him both in bed and out.

She seemed to be trapped in a daze, their hands still connected. Her gray eyes were full of desire, but he could see she was trying to suppress it.

"Hi," she said finally.

He could tell by her ashen face that she was only going to get out the one word and nothing else. Her full lips quivered, and he longed to haul her into his arms and kiss her, perhaps bite those lips playfully until she smiled again.

Why wasn't she like every other girl he'd slept with? They'd been forgotten the moment they'd left his bed. A parade of pretty faces and nothing more. But he knew every freckle on Kat's face, every curve of her tempting body, how her mouth felt as she'd explored his skin, eager, and yet new to the experience of sex. How could he ever forget being with her? There was no way he'd give her up, not when there was so much left to discover between them.

They were both damned now.

"I'll show Katherine to a guest room. You and Clayton can plan the evening while I see her settled," Tristan offered, needing, *hoping* for one minute alone with her.

"Excellent idea, Tristan." His mother's beaming face made his body flood with a dark tide of guilt.

All he wanted was to talk to her. They needed a plan. Neither of their parents could ever find out they'd slept together. They had to keep everything secret.

"Follow me, Kat." He almost reached for her hand, but caught himself just inches from her wrist.

Pulling back his arm, he forced himself to keep his distance.

"Thank you, Tristan." Kat's father smiled, too, curling an arm around Lizzy's waist.

Tristan swallowed hard and nodded, but didn't linger. He didn't want to endure public displays of affection involving his mother. *Too bloody awkward.*

Kat followed him out of the drawing room, closing the door behind her. The second the door was shut he grabbed her hand, wild inside with the need to touch her. He knew they shouldn't continue this... whatever it was between them, but right now, as he held her hand, none of that mattered.

To hell with our parents. I want her.

"Tristan," she whispered, her breath catching as he pulled her down the hall to the stairs that led to the upper floors.

"This way."

"Where are we going?" she asked as they climbed the steps.

"Somewhere we can talk," he muttered and tugged her into the nearest guest bedroom.

The instant they were alone inside the room, he shoved her against the closed door and gave in to his desire. Kissing her hard, he unleashed an explosion of lust and need that had made him hard the moment he'd seen her in the drawing room. He delved into her mouth, seeking her tongue, and she met him boldly, her lips just as eager. He caught her wrists and jerked them above her head, pinning them with one hand.

It felt so bloody good to kiss her again. How sweet she tasted, how soft and feminine she felt against his body. God, he'd missed this, and he'd only been without her a few days. Using his other hand, he stroked down her side, cupped her round arse, making her hips buck against his touch.

It had only been two days since they'd parted

from his room in Cambridge. Two bloody days that had felt like an eternity without Kat in his arms. He'd wanted to see her before he left for London, but he'd had to leave right away. Fuck, he needed to take her here, right now, against the door.

Panting, he rocked against her, relishing the little sounds of pleasure she made when he used his body to cage hers while they kissed. Each time his lips touched hers, he fell deeper into a trance of pleasure that silenced the world outside their shared breaths. There was never enough; he would always crave her with this wild madness. The American knew just what to do with her pink little tongue to make his cock ache...

I'm going to lose my fucking mind.

Their mouths finally parted, and Tristan rested his forehead against hers, his eyes closed as he relished the control he had over her and the closeness of their bodies. It would be so easy to ravish her right here; she wanted it, too. The little minx was staring up at him with those silver-gray eyes, like polished moon-stones gleaming with lust. The shivers racking her body made him all the more hungry to take her right there, but it was too much of a risk with their parents so close. Lord, he hated how clear that one thought was. Their parents were downstairs talking about wedding plans, and he was up here, ready to take his future stepsister to bed. Talk about scandalous. Sure, they weren't blood related, but most people would turn a disapproving eye on this situation.

When he opened his eyes, he saw tears on Kat's cheeks.

Tears?

Confusion jolted though him like an electric shock. He dropped his hand from her wrists, and she lowered her arms, wrapping them around herself.

"Kat, darling, what's the matter?" He lifted a

hand to touch her cheek, but she shied away and darted around him. When she put the bed between them, something hard knotted in his stomach. "Kat?"

"Tristan, how long have you known?" she demanded.

"Known what?"

"About our parents. How long have you known they were dating?" Silent accusations glittered in her eyes.

Kat thought he'd kept that from her? His heart kicked against his ribs. He wouldn't lie to her, she *had* to know that. Tristan was many things, but a liar wasn't one of them.

"I *didn't* know, I swear to you. Not until you walked in the door, and Mother said your name. I only knew my mother's new fiancé had a daughter. She never mentioned a name. Kat, the odds of this happening..." He gestured around them. "That our parents would get together?" He began to pace, unable to stand still with all the pent-up energy crackling inside him. "Honestly, Kat, I didn't know." He paused, facing her.

Those damnable tears still covered her cheeks. There was nothing worse than watching a woman cry. He couldn't stop it, couldn't undo whatever had hurt her. Moving toward her again, he reached out to cup her shoulders. Kat dodged his grasp.

"Why won't you let me touch you?" That look of hurt in her eyes was killing him, and he couldn't explain why. He needed to hold her.

"Tristan, our parents are *engaged*. Don't you get it? We can't be together. If my dad ever found us like this, he'd freak out. This has to stop."

Stop? He couldn't let her go. There was no chance of that.

"No, I—"

"I mean it, Tristan. I won't jeopardize my father's happiness. Not for good sex."

"Great sex," he corrected.

Her little smile in response was melancholy. "Great sex. It's not going to happen again. Do you understand?" Her cheeks flushed, and her chin lifted in a show of strength. It was one of the things he loved about her, how strong she was, but he didn't want her strong now, not when she was resisting what lay between them.

"I can handle your father, Kat," he promised. "They would never have to know we're together." If Kat wanted to be with him, he would find a way to keep it a secret from their parents.

She drew in a fortifying breath and pulled her hair back from her face as she exhaled.

"It will only end badly. No matter what happens. They can never know about us, and we can't *ever* do what we did again. We're going to be brother and sister. Even if it's just stepsiblings, that's still...not okay. People will talk, and I don't want that. Tell me you understand, and that you agree we have to stay away from each other."

No. Every instinct inside him was shouting to deny her request. What they'd shared couldn't be abandoned and couldn't be thrown away just because it was forbidden.

"Kat, I want *you.* What happened between us, that doesn't happen every day." He took a step toward her, but she held up a hand.

Those tears shimmered like diamonds on her skin. Beautiful and shattering at the same time.

"Please, just go. I need some time alone."

Alone? How was she going to be alone at a time like this? They were all trapped in the same house for three weeks. He didn't want to leave her so she could cry by herself. He knew that was what she was going to do; the pain of her decision to end things between them was all over her face. Just like the last time, when she'd told him to get out of her dorm room.

Tristan weighed the options of trying to kiss her again, or at least hold her, but it didn't seem likely he'd succeed. She'd raised her chin, and her kissable lips were set in a firm line. It would be better if he waited. Gave her time to breathe. Once she'd had time to cool off, he'd be able to reason with her. He didn't like the idea of patience, but he sensed that if he pressed her now he might lose her. And he couldn't lose her, not again.

"Very well," he said, backing away. But it was a long moment before he was able to compose himself. He paused after opening the door. "Please don't push me away, Kat."

She didn't look at him. That hit him like a punch to the gut. Stepping outside, he closed her door and leaned back against it. Tristan tilted his head back, staring at the ceiling.

"Tristan." A masculine voice jerked him from his thoughts.

Kat's father was standing there, hands in his pockets, watching him, his gaze penetrating. He was a man, Tristan thought, who would easily figure out if his daughter was being seduced by his future stepson.

If Tristan wanted to get Kat beneath him on a bed he'd have to be very stealthy.

"Mr. Roberts." He nodded in greeting.

"Is my daughter all right?" Clayton asked, his brows knitted together. He walked up to Tristan, and Tristan had a distinct impression the other man was measuring him up, while trying not to make his observations too overt. Just as Tristan was doing.

"She's a bit overwhelmed, I believe." Not a lie exactly.

Clayton Roberts cleared his throat and shuffled

his shoes on the carpet. "Ahh, I knew this would be a shock to her and I should've waited for all of this, given her more time, but..." He paused and raised his head. "I love your mother very much and didn't *want* to wait."

The man was open and honest, and Tristan couldn't hate him for that. His mother had lived a hellish existence while married to his father. She deserved a good man, one who would love her the way his father had failed to.

"Then you'd better take good care of her." It wasn't a threat, but he'd be happy to make it one if Clayton didn't.

The American simply laughed. Did they always act so odd about such serious things? Kat certainly did.

"I will," Clayton promised. "It's not every day a man is given a second chance at happiness."

"Good." Tristan didn't really know what to say. He felt awkward talking to this stranger who would become his stepfather. He was used to being in a position of power around other men, but this wasn't a situation he could have prepared for.

Fucking hell. When Carter found out about this... His best friend would laugh clear through next week.

"I'll check on Kat," Clayton said, offering a warm but hesitant smile. "Why don't you let your mother know we'll be down for dinner later?"

"I will," Tristan replied. With a sinking feeling deep in his chest he walked away from Kat's door.

CHAPTER 2

K at sat on her bed, knees tucked up to her chest, arms curled around her shins. Tears dripped down her cheeks, soaking her jeans in two little damp patches on her knees. Everything inside her was a jumbled mess of pain and confusion, all of it so thick and strangling she could barely breathe.

Dad's engaged, and my future stepbrother is Tristan Kingsley. My Tristan.

Two weeks ago I saw him walk into a pub and kissed him because I wanted to experience an adventure. Two days ago I gave him my virginity, and we shared the most mindblowing sex ever. Now he's here...and he's going to be part of my family.

I'm so screwed.

It didn't change how she felt about him. He was gorgeous, not just on the outside, but inside, too. Their first night together, he'd confessed things, small whispers in the dark about himself. What filled him with joy, made his heart beat fast. Things a man wouldn't share unless he really wanted to. He'd opened up to her, and she'd done the same in return.

That has to mean something doesn't it?

He was sexy, addictive, so electric in bed that he'd

left her more spellbound with every kiss, every caress. Everyone said having sex for the first time would be painful, awkward, and unsatisfying. Not with Tristan. He'd fulfilled every fantasy she'd ever had. The dark brooding bad boy, one who dominated her senses with his mouth, his exploring hands, his power over her, yet never making her feel she couldn't tell him no if she wasn't ready. They'd made love all night in his bed at the grand Fox Hill estate while the snow fell outside the windows. All she had needed was him. Nothing else had mattered.

Kat closed her eyes, still feeling his hands around her wrists, the way he'd pinned her against the door. It made her body flush with heat and her blood pound in her ears. How did he know just what to do to make her unravel from the inside out? Why couldn't she go back to Cambridge and his bed where it was just the two of them? She needed him to touch her, to make her feel alive, to show her that exquisite world of pleasure he'd only given her a taste of two days ago.

But now I can't have him. He's going to be my step-brother.

It didn't get any more off-limits than that. Her dad would freak out if he ever found out she and Tristan had... She shook her head. Clayton had always been protective, and he'd never approve of her dating someone older than she was. And Tristan was twenty-five to her nineteen. A six-year difference.

God, this was so bad, so bad. She didn't want to think about how she'd have to spend not just this Christmas but all holidays to come around him and survive not being with him. Because if she was being totally honest with herself...it wasn't just her dad finding out that scared her. It was how easy it would be to fall in love with Tristan. The more time they spent together, the harder it became to go their separate ways. Love was dangerous. Love burned a person up inside. She'd watched it destroy her father's life after her mother had left.

I don't ever want that to happen to me.

The thought of that agonizing pain, that awful crushing of one's heart...it was something she never wanted to experience. But Tristan had the power to do that to her. She'd gotten her heart involved when she opened herself up to him and shared parts of herself she'd never shared with anyone else. And he'd shared himself right back. Still, she feared he wouldn't feel the same way about her. A man like Tristan didn't fall in love; he had too many woman out there to seduce, and she was just his current obsession, God only knew why.

Sniffling, she wiped her hands across her cheeks, trying to get rid of her tears. Maybe her dad getting married to Lizzy was a good thing. Tristan being off-limits as a stepbrother would make it easier for her to stay away from him. It would protect her heart. She'd had her adventure, she'd slept with him and almost fallen in love. It was as close as she could allow herself to get without risking her heart.

I just have to find a way to steer clear of him for three weeks. No matter how hard it is, I have to resist him.

Kat closed her eyes, memories of him flooding her until she couldn't ignore them.

Every time she'd see his hands, she'd remember how he had pressed her down on the mattress as he hovered over her body. She had to watch his mouth as he spoke and not think of the sinful way those lips had sucked on the tips of her breasts, or how he'd licked her in secret places that had made her scream his name until she was hoarse. He had shown her that pleasure wasn't just physical. Every time they'd been close, not just in bed, she'd felt alive, as though every part of her body and soul reached out to his, connecting them. His laughter had filled her heart, and his flirty smile had stolen her breath. And she couldn't forget the way he had looked at her when they first met, as if there'd been no one else in the room...

The guestroom door opened, and her father's head appeared around the edge. She jerked, her face flaming. *Thank God he couldn't hear her thoughts.*

"Hey, honey, mind if I come in for a minute?"

Her day couldn't get any worse. "Sure." She shifted to sit cross-legged as her dad closed the door and walked over to sit on the bed.

He ran his hand through his dark hair and sighed. There was a weariness in his eyes that hadn't been there moments before.

I've done that to him. I wasn't happy about this whole engagement thing.

Sure she could fake some smiles and politeness, but her father knew her better than that. Guilt gnawed at her insides, and she fought the sting of fresh tears in her eyes. It was selfish to want him all to herself and to have Tristan all to herself, too. And she hated herself for that.

Her father eased down on the bed beside her, his large hand touching hers, familiar and comforting.

"Come here, honey," he murmured.

She moved closer, and he wrapped an arm around her shoulders, making her lean over so he could press a kiss to her forehead and hug her tightly. In that moment, hurting the way she was, she felt as if she were twelve years old. She was supposed to be mature for her age, not prone to crying or acting out. She wanted to be an adult in her father's eyes, not a child needing protection. More important, she wanted to be a woman whom someone like Tristan would admire and respect. Even though they couldn't be together, she still wanted him to like her.

"I screwed up. I realize that. I should have told you about Lizzy much sooner." He rubbed her arm in the rough-but-gentle way only fathers seemed to manage.

Kat sat there, numb inside, as she listened to his deep, rumbling voice. For so long it had been just the two of them. Her mother had bailed on them once she'd realized how hard parenthood would be, and Kat's father had spent the last ten years proving that they hadn't needed her. That the two of them could do just fine on their own.

Everything was going to change now. And Tristan as her new stepbrother? It was so messed up she couldn't even think about it without a throbbing pulse beating right behind her eyes.

"Kat, please talk to me," her father begged. "It's okay if you're upset or angry, but don't shut me out." He gave her shoulder a little pat.

Where would I even begin? "Hey, Dad, I'm so glad you just up and decided to marry some woman without talking to me. Oh, and by the way, I totally slept with my future stepbrother, but that's cool, right?* Yeah, her dad might have a heart attack.

"I know it's a lot to take in," Clayton said.

"You just dumped this on me, and I can't be instantly happy for you." The comment slipped out, crueler than she meant it.

"I'm sorry, Kat. I wish you could understand. The last several years have been...lonely for me. When your mother left, I gave up being happy." He turned his face away, his chin dropping silently. "I was convinced I'd never love again, *could* never love again. She was my first love, Kat. It's not easy to get over losing that."

An image of Tristan, smiling, holding her in bed flashed across her mind.

She crushed that thought, grinding it to dust. That was lust. Pure and simple. *Not love*.

"When you fall in love for the first time everything is new and exciting, sometimes scary. It's all fire and love and passion. If that fire goes out, the cold that follows... It scars you, soul deep."

Kat stared at her father, her own heart splintering inside her chest as she watched him bare his soul to her. They'd never talked about her mother. *Never*.

"I'm sorry, Dad," she whispered and leaned into him, resting her head on his shoulder. He put his arm around her again.

"It's not your fault. It took me ten years to learn that it wasn't *us* she left. It was the concept of a family that troubled her. It meant she had to be a part of our team. And that's what families are. A team." He finally looked down at her again and smiled. "I want you to be open to adding Lizzy and Tristan to our team, our family. I know you don't know them yet, but I think you'll like them."

Kat winced. She couldn't confess just how well she did know Tristan.

She rubbed her palms on her jeans before looking at him. "How did you know you loved her?"

"Your mother?"

With a little shake of her head, she dropped her gaze again. "Lizzy. How did you know?"

Clayton grinned, and the expression lit up his entire face. When had he ever looked so happy? Not in a *long* time. The man had put the *work* in workaholic. He claimed he never had time for dating, yet Lizzy had changed that *and* him. Kat wanted to know what had pushed her father to act so out of character. She needed to understand why he'd want to take a risk with his heart again after what had happened when her mother had left.

"She makes me smile. When we first met, she *saw*

me, just me. Not my money, not my job. It's so easy to talk to her, she listens, and I love to listen back. It's something I never had with your mother. An openness of the heart we were both missing in our first marriages. Neither of us expected or planned this, but it happened, and I can't imagine life without her now." Her father tilted her chin back and studied her face. "Someday you'll fall in love, and it will change you forever."

Kat thought of monarch butterflies and the way the caterpillars formed chrysalises and then, after a period of time, were reborn. They could never go back to being caterpillars. Falling in love was a type of metamorphosis. But it was a dangerous one, for her heart.

"She makes you happy?" Kat asked, even though she knew the answer.

"Yes, very happy."

Kat ducked her head. So Lizzy was here to stay because she made Dad happy. That meant Tristan wasn't going anywhere anytime soon and he was definitely going to be her stepbrother. How in the hell was she going to survive the holidays?

"Now, will you join us for our first family dinner in a couple of hours, after you settle in?"

"Yes." She could do that. Dinner would be easy. All she had to do was eat, right? Then why did the very thought of it make her stomach turn?

"Good." Her father rose from her bed and kissed her forehead again. "I'll see you in a bit."

"Uh-huh." She waited until he'd gone before she threw herself back upon the bed and stared up at the four-poster bed hangings over her head.

She had to admit, Lizzy had excellent taste in interior design. The town house was beautiful. Just like Fox Hill, Lizzy's house in Cambridge. Everything the woman touched was perfect. Just like Tristan. He had that same golden touch his mother had when it came to beautiful things and beautiful houses. Like his bedroom at Fox Hill. And his bed... That thought led to other thoughts of them in that bed, bodies entwined, sharing moans and breathless whispers.

Oh no, I can't go there.

I just need to survive dinner and lie low. If I avoid Tristan, he'll give up and leave me alone. I'll be able to forget about our mind-blowing perfect night together, and we won't break up our parents' marriage. And I won't let him carve his name in my heart.

That invisible pressure of his hands on her body was there again, haunting her, lingering in her mind and her senses. She shivered. "Damn it."

CHAPTER 3

"Tristan." His mother's call halted him in his tracks on the way to his bedroom.

"Hello, Mum," he said as he spotted her at the end of the hall near the doorway to the small upstairs study.

"Might I have a quick word?" She rubbed her palms together nervously.

Shoving his hands into his pockets, he walked over to her and followed her into the study.

She closed the door behind them and faced him. "I know we haven't talked much tonight, but now we have a chance." She waited, biting her lip and smoothing her hands over her white cashmere sweater.

"I'm happy to talk, Mum." He would humor her, but he wasn't going to start this conversation.

"Well, what do you think of them? Kat seems like a lovely girl. Clayton says she's shy, but a wonderful student. Did you know she's attending Cambridge, just like you? She's only a freshman, but maybe you will have a chance to see her when you both return after holiday."

He almost smiled. Tristan planned on doing just

that, seeing lots of Kat *in his bed*. Preferably with her ankles thrown over his shoulders and her sweet cries of ecstasy filling his ears as she begged him to fuck her harder. He cleared his throat and attempted to put that delicious thought on hold.

"They seem very nice, Mum. I hope you've thought this through, though. Father won't be pleased…" He walked over to one of the couches and stretched out on it.

"Let me worry about your father. And yes, I *have* thought this through. I want you to like Clayton and Kat." Lizzy took a chair opposite him. "It's important to me that you do. We're going to be a family, Tristan. He and I want to spend the rest of our lives together."

Tristan folded his arms over his abdomen and met his mother's concerned gaze. "Does he make you happy?"

A warm, unguarded smile touched her lips. "He does. And he makes me laugh. I didn't know love could be like that. With your father…" A red blush stained her cheeks, and she turned her face toward the window. Weak winter light penetrated the thick panes of glass and illuminated her hair, bringing out the hints of red amid the darker brown.

"You don't need to talk about him, Mum." He drummed his fingers on his stomach.

"I know." She laughed softly, a mixture of chagrin and amusement in her tone that made him smile. It had been too long since he'd heard her sound so content. If Kat's dad made his mother laugh, that was a good thing.

With a sigh of resignation, she faced him. "We do need to talk about your father, though. He's demanded that you be at the estate for Christmas. We both know how he gets when you don't do what he wants."

Her words drew forth a quarter-century of dark memories. Cold holidays, icy dinners, frosty exchanges over afternoon tea. Never a kind word, never a single utterance of praise or affection. And always that knowledge that his father's word was law. Whatever the old boy wished, it had to be done, or else someone would pay dearly for defying his orders.

The Earl of Pembroke was an absolutely wretched human being and an even worse husband and father. It was no surprise that the local papers in London loved to drag out any negative news about him when they could. Usually they used Tristan to do it, smearing the papers with photos of affairs and lovers, trying to tie him to his father and his father's political agenda in the House of Lords.

"You'll talk to him, won't you?" his mother asked. "Smooth things over for Christmas?"

"I'll call him tomorrow. He won't get more than a few days from me, though."

His mother's smile wilted at the corners. "Be careful, Tristan." She cleared her throat and then changed the subject. "How's Carter doing?"

Tristan shrugged. "Carter is well. Still in love with Celia."

"He is such a delightful young man. If only her parents weren't so opposed to him."

Indeed. Parental opposition was the death of many relationships in a society like his. The peerage of Britain had standards, and they forced them to be met, albeit quite secretly. A relationship with Kat, for example, would be permitted as a temporary dalliance, but never a marriage.

Not that he intended to marry Kat—she was only nineteen and far too young to marry anyone—but when he did marry, his father was going to attempt to pick his bride as though they were stuck in the Victorian Age. Therefore, he had every intention of delaying marriage to anyone as along as possible. He wanted to enjoy his bachelor years while he could, which included being with Kat. He was going to have Kat in his bed again, and he wouldn't let something like his father's disapproval slice through what lay between them. If they had to build a world of secrets to keep their relationship hidden, he would do whatever was necessary to have her. He'd give her some time, some space...but he would get her back in his bed, right where she belonged.

Just when I thought life didn't challenge me anymore... He chuckled.

"What's amused you, sweetheart?" His mother raised one elegant brow. As a boy, that tone and questioning gaze had made him confess many sins. Now he was made of sterner stuff.

"I was merely thinking of Carter and Celia." He rarely lied to his mother, but this was necessary.

If she ever learned of his interest in Kat, his mother could upset all his plans. She would swoop in and carry Kat away to safety, far out of his reach. She'd never been blind to his activities. Along with most of London, she'd seen him in the papers and knew his levels of debauchery.

"You know," his mother paused, "you should give Kat a tour of the house tonight." His mother rose from her chair, resting one hand on the top of the wingback. "I want her to feel comfortable here. After we get married, they'll be moving in, since Clayton's flat is too tiny for all of us. Besides"—his mother sighed wistfully—"I love this house. It's a relief Clayton doesn't mind my choosing my place over his."

Tristan wondered how Kat would feel about moving in here during the school holidays. He remembered that night in Kat's dorm room when she'd explained why she loved books so much and how she'd never had a place to settle down for long. They were friends she could take with her, she'd said, friends she'd never had to say good-bye to. She'd confessed this in the dim, warm confines of her little bed that first night, when they'd slept together without sex. Even though he'd wanted to bed her more than anything, he'd bided his time, enjoyed feeling her in his arms, controlling their first foray into the land of pleasure without actually getting inside her body the way he'd wanted most.

He'd wound his arms around her, and something deep in his chest had twisted painfully as he listened to her open her heart. It hadn't lessened the raging lust to possess this girl, but it had softened that animal hunger, deepened it... He'd held her closer, tighter, wanting to ease his ache and her own. Unable to resist getting close to her, he'd shared with her his love of maps, and the way stained glass filled him with strong, powerful emotions.

Yes, there was much he and Kat had yet to learn about each other, but he would make sure they would have the time.

He'd never wanted to be with just one woman before, but he was starting to see the appeal of having a relationship of some kind with her. The more he learned about Kat, the more she learned about him, the more intense their bed play was. He craved the way bedding her made him feel. Powerful, exhilarated, uninhibited, and completely free, yet bound to her at the same time.

I need to be careful. My taking Kat to bed could ruin my mother's happiness.

Tristan sat up on the couch and studied his mother. When his father had left the pair of them alone for weeks at a time while he'd seen to his duties on the estate or handled matters in Parliament, she'd brought Tristan to Fox Hill. After he'd grown up, she'd started spending more time in London at the town house she'd acquired after the divorce. It offered her a way to stay in the middle of town and not feel so isolated while she rebuilt her life.

He'd grown to love this house and Fox Hill as much as she did. For his mother to suggest that someone besides him would live here was her way of opening up and showing the world she was ready to live, now that love was back in her life. Tristan couldn't help but admire her.

"Promise me you'll be nice to Kat. Clayton says she doesn't have many friends because they've moved so often. Neither of them are used to this way of living either, with cooks, servants, and drivers. As her older brother—"

"*Stepbrother*," he cut in. That distinction was vitally important, given what he planned to do to her in his bed.

"Er...yes," his mother nodded. "Stepbrother. She would benefit from having someone like you to show her London and introduce her to people. It would be perfect during the holidays to take her to see all the sights."

"I think that is a lovely idea, Mum." He grinned so broadly that his cheeks hurt as he leaned back into the couch and crossed his hands behind his head.

Take Kat about London? His mother had unwittingly provided him the perfect way to slowly entice Kat back into his bed. He'd have to pretend he had no intention of seducing her, though. He would play the polite, friendly stepbrother she wanted him to be. For now.

You will be mine again, sweet Kat.

KAT HAD JUST STEPPED OUT OF THE SHOWER AND

wrapped a towel around her body when she heard the doorknob rattle.

"Just a minute!" It was probably her dad trying to check on her.

The brass knob rattled again.

"Almost done," she said as she tucked the towel more firmly about her body, mentally smacking herself for forgetting to pack her long robe.

When she unlocked the door, it flew open instantly. A shirtless Tristan stood there, holding a towel, looking down at her with those hypnotic blue-green eyes.

Her eyes, without approval from her brain, swept down over his body: the sculpted abs, the indentations of his pelvic muscles, and the way his jeans hung low on his hips. Hips she'd held and dug her nails into the other night as he'd pounded into her. Her lower body twisted and clenched with sudden desire at the mere memory of his raw, powerful possession of her. She couldn't forget the feel of his body, pressing her down, his cock filling her until she couldn't breathe. The way he'd *owned* every part of her.

Damn. How had she convinced herself that avoiding him was a good idea? Right now she wanted to drop the towel and beg him to take her, damn the consequences.

"Are you finished?" His tone was pleasant. No hint of fire, no branding scorch of his gaze...just politeness. He was doing exactly what she'd asked him to do. Treat her like a stepsister he'd only just met. Before today's awful revelation of their parents' engagement, he would have smirked at her, teased, and tried to steal the towel... A pang of longing for the playful part of him swept through her. God, she missed that.

What would it take to win one little smile from him, one that was meant for her, and not tempered by his polite distance.

I asked for this. It didn't make her feel any better.

"I'm done." Heat rushed to her face from embarrassment at her inner thoughts. Thankfully he had *no idea* how conflicted she was feeling right now. Or how her body was reacting to being so close to him and being denied his touch. Like a thirsty woman crawling across a Saharan desert and glimpsing an island oasis only to discover it was a mirage.

He made a low, gruff noise, not exactly a response, but it sent shivers through her. She couldn't forget the sounds he'd made in bed two nights ago. He'd been half-animal, growling, nipping, showing her a rough side to passion, one she knew she would always crave. Tristan had pierced a dark part of her sexual side, exposing it to the light, and she couldn't deny that it existed, nor did she *want* to.

He slid past her, their bodies brushed in the narrow space of the doorway. Heat exploded through her, and she froze, trying to control her reaction to him.

Tristan froze, too, their bodies pressed close. His warm breath fanned her cheeks and his natural masculine scent enveloped her. Memories of their night together came flooding back, no matter how she tried to keep it out.

He lifted his hand to her cheek, pausing a second before he would have touched her. She met his gaze, her breaths shallow as his lips twitched in a ghost of a smile. Then he brushed his knuckles over her skin. Fire rippled in the wake of that "barely there" caress. Every part of her was aware of him and his closeness.

Would it be so hard to keep a relationship between them a secret from their parents? Maybe they could...

"Please..." she begged, unsure of what she really wanted.

"Please, what?" he replied, in that dark, low tone

that made her purr inside like a cat in heat. He slowly backed her into the wall next to the shower, closing the door behind him. He placed his hands on either side of her head, caging her in, and lowered his face to hers.

A feather-light, teasing kiss. A nip at her bottom lip. She clenched her thighs together, feeling the rush of wet heat in response to his subtle aggression. How could he affect her like this? His touch, his kiss, sent her body into riotous waves of longing for him.

He nuzzled her neck, licking and nibbling on the sensitive spots that sent electric pulses from her head to her toes.

Kat grabbed his shoulders, digging her fingers into his hot, bare skin. The towel around her body stretched against her breasts as she struggled to control her breathing.

His hands dropped from the wall to her waist, tugging on the folds of the towel that barely covered her.

It would be so easy, he could lift my towel up and fuck me right here against the wall. Just one more time, we could...

The towel dropped to the floor.

Tristan's eyes raked over her naked body, and when he lifted his head and met her gaze, one corner of his mouth slid into a lazy half-grin that hit her so hard her knees knocked together.

He lifted one finger, pressed it to his lips, and made a soft "Shhh" before he leaned down to kiss her collarbone. Her nipples pebbled with the cool air and her building arousal. She stared down at the top of Tristan's head, noting the way the light brought out hints of copper in the dark locks. His kisses traveled down in a slow, teasing path to one of her breasts. When he flicked his tongue against one sensitive peak, a whimper escaped her.

He is going to kill me. Right here in the bathroom of his mother's house... *Holy fuck*...

Her hands moved to grip his hair, but he caught her wrists and pinned them against the wall by her hips.

"Oh, God," she panted as he knelt in front of her and glanced up, that wicked grin curving his lips upward. There was no denying the magnetic pull of that smile and how it obliterated all of her defenses.

Tristan lifted one of her legs up, putting her calf over his shoulder, opening her to him. Kat dug her nails into the wall, praying she could keep her balance. Tristan's lips danced lightly down from her navel to her mound. His lips settled around her clit, which pulsed hard and sharp. The tip of his tongue stroked, flicked, and played with the swollen bud. As he teased her with his mouth, his hand coasted up her inner thigh before it found her wet entrance. Drawing lazy, slow patterns in her tender flesh, Tristan tortured her with exquisite agony. Kat squirmed, writhed, pleaded in little soft desperate sounds for him to stop, to keep going...to...

"Ahh!" Kat gasped as he licked at her.

The pulsating sense of need, was too great to deny. The explosive climax hit her hard, and she threw her head back, swallowing her cry of pleasure when his hands dug into her ass, holding her in place while he drew out her orgasm, lapping at her folds until she was too sensitive to do anything but beg for mercy. Currents of desire rippled through her, not diminished at all by the fact that she'd just come apart with his mouth on her.

The wicked glint in Tristan's eyes was her only warning that he had no intention of stopping. He started to dip his head toward her mound again with a throaty chuckle.

"*Please*..." she rasped frantically, dying to have him

take her. It didn't matter what happened outside the door, they were here together and he was going to...

"Kat?" Her father knocked on the bathroom door.

She sucked in a breath, and Tristan's hands, which were stroking her outer thighs, stilled, his muscles tensing beneath her palms. Neither of them moved. Neither of them dared to breathe. Her heart pounded so hard that she couldn't hear anything outside of that thunderous racing beat in her ears.

"Kat, are you okay?" her father asked, rapping his knuckles on the door again.

Tristan rose silently to his feet to tower over her again. His blue-green eyes cut through her as he stared down at her. "Answer him, before he opens the door." It was barely a whisper but she was close enough to hear him.

She cleared her throat, her mouth dry. "I'm fine, Dad. Be out in a few minutes." She closed her eyes, praying her dad wouldn't break the first rule of the father-daughter code and come inside without her express permission.

"Okay, honey."

Her ears strained to pick up on the sounds of his departure. When several seconds had passed, she sagged against the wall, letting go of Tristan's arms. Then she dove for the bath towel and flung it around her body.

"We can't do this again." She met his gaze, surprised at the flicker of anger in his eyes.

His sensual, full lips thinned into a hard line, and his eyes narrowed, the fire in them dimming. His jaw clenched, and he turned his face away as though he didn't want to look at her. He was mad, and she couldn't blame him. They'd lost control right here in the bathroom because the magnetic pull between them was too strong. Sexual frustration coursed through her, and she bit her lip, focusing on the sting of pain to get her mind off of how much she wished she had surrendered to him completely and how he'd have been deep inside her right now if she had.

He moved away to pull a towel from a rack above the toilet and dropped it on the counter. Then he glanced over his shoulder.

"Mum has asked me to give you a tour of the house so you'll know where everything is while you're here. I'll meet you outside your room in half an hour." Then he turned to face the shower.

As he leaned into the stall and flicked the faucet handle to turn the water on, Kat watched the muscles of his back play in little ripples. The faintest trace of claw marks still cut across his shoulder blades. *Her* marks. Again, that flood of primal desire and animal satisfaction moved through her. She wanted to make more, to permanently claim this gorgeous man as hers.

But he's not mine, not anymore. I can't have him because it will put our parents, and my heart, at risk. That last part was her deepest fear. She'd started to care about him, to get addicted to him, not just physically but emotionally. She didn't want to get her heart broken. She'd grown up watching her father live with a shattered heart and she didn't want that to happen to her. What if she wasn't strong enough to survive that level of heartache?

The sound of his pants zipper had her jolting back to awareness and hastily ducking out of the bathroom. The last thing she needed was to catch a glimpse of him in anything less than jeans. After how he'd just gone down on her, she was having a hard time convincing herself she shouldn't want to return the favor... Her libido and self-control couldn't handle that. Flushing guiltily, she clutched her towel around her body and dashed back to her room. How was she going to get through this? With Tristan sleeping just down the hall, naked, the way he'd told her he did...

Shit, I'm in too deep here. I want him too much... How am I going to survive three weeks with him being so close?

WHAT TO KNOW WHAT HAPPENS NEXT? GRAB Seduction HERE!

ABOUT THE AUTHOR

USA TODAY Bestselling Author Lauren Smith is an Oklahoma attorney by day, who pens adventurous and edgy romance stories by the light of her smart phone flashlight app. She knew she was destined to be a romance writer when she attempted to re-write the entire _Titanic_ movie just to save Jack from drowning. Connecting with readers by writing emotionally moving, realistic and sexy romances no matter what time period is her passion. She's won multiple awards in several romance sub-genres including: New England Reader's Choice Awards, Greater Detroit BookSeller's Best Awards, and a Semi-Finalist award for the Mary Wollstonecraft Shelley Award.

To connect with Lauren, visit her at:
www.laurensmithbooks.com
lauren@Laurensmithbooks.com

 facebook.com/LaurenDianaSmith

twitter.com/LSmithAuthor

instagram.com/LaurenSmithbooks

bookbub.com/authors/lauren-smith